PATRICIA A. BREMMER

Dolphins'

Echo

Sequel to

"Tryst with Dolphins"

Patricia A. Bremmer

ISBN 0-9745884-1-5

For additional copies contact:

Windcall Enterprises

75345 Road 317
Venango, NE 69168
308-447-5571

ACKNOWLEDGEMENTS

My thanks and acknowledgement to all that encouraged and helped me to create **"Dolphins' Echo"**.

Debbie Karst, for her assistance in developing the character of Detective Karst.

Detective Glen Karst, used his expertise in his field to keep my crime scenes believable.

Kent Walters, for allowing me to invade his quiet space to write.

Joni and Sarah Lawver, for their help as editors.

Jack Sommars, screenplay writer, for all his comments, suggestions and criticisms.

Mark Hofmann, a friend, his lifestyle proved to be sheer inspiration once again.

To all of my readers that begged for more!

Chapter 1

That morning, Ashley slowly awoke to the sound of doves cooing outside her bedroom window. She lay in bed listening to the song of the gentle birds. That was the special morning Ashley had scheduled for her ultrasound. She held both hands over her stomach. It showed no real signs of growth yet. She was anxiously awaiting the changes her body was about to undergo.

Her mood saddened as she spoke to her unborn child, "I feel so badly that your dad won't be here to share today with us."

Michael, Ashley's husband, had died from an asthma attack six weeks earlier. To all concerned it appeared to have been an accident but Ashley and the rest knew it was murder. The rest consisted of four of Ashley's friends from high school.

She thought back to that terrible night of the slumber party last December. If only she hadn't felt so guilty about dropping Theresa from their little clique of friends. When the five of them went away to college, they had left her behind pregnant by Mark. If only she had not agreed to call all of the group back together to have that adult slumber party. If only they hadn't played that game of how to murder a husband, Michael and the others would be alive today.

Ashley often played this whatif game in her mind, blaming herself for the deaths of five husbands. The only relief she got from remembering everything that had happened over the last few months was from the knowledge that Theresa was dead. Theresa was the insane person who killed all of the husbands. She failed with her last attempt to kill her own husband, Mark. She died instead.

All of the murders were planned so carefully that each was treated as an accident except for Amy's husband, Jonathon. That was set up to look like the husband of a lover killed him. Thank goodness that husband did not do any prison time. The jury could not convict him because there was a reasonable doubt.

If that man had been convicted the girls, or Dolphins as they were nicknamed from their high school swim team, would have been forced to go to the police with their story. Spending time in prison was not in their plan for their futures.

The night of the slumber party the girls began innocently discussing Amy's husband and his many affairs.

Stephanie, one of the Dolphins, blurted out, "If my husband ever decided to have an affair and I found out about it I'd kill him."

Amy, a criminal attorney, asked, "Yeah, and just how would you go about such a thing when all of his friends are lawyers and most of them into criminal law?"

Ashley remembered explaining to the five other women at the party that it would be extremely difficult to pull off the perfect murder. Research done by Ashley for her murder mystery novels convinced her that most murders could be solved. Those that are not have some clue that has been overlooked or has not yet surfaced.

The conversation ignited something in Theresa. She was already a bit over the edge. She came up with the great idea to plot the murder of Jonathon in such a way that it would be a perfect crime. She suggested Ashley use the plot and all of the details for one of her books. Then Theresa took the entire thing one step further and had everyone add to the plot of not just Jonathon's murder but the murder of each of their husbands based on one annoying attribute that each husband harbored in his own personality.

It was not very difficult to get a group of women that had too much to drink to spill their guts about what their husbands did to annoy them. Ashley would tell them when the plots were not feasible or had been overdone. Amy would help by explaining how to get around police procedure.

3

Brittany, the model, had the most difficulty playing this slumber party game. Brittany with her soft blue eyes and white blond hair had the most sensitive personality. The game actually brought her to tears and she didn't want to play any longer, but Theresa forced the issue explaining they must all be accomplices.

How sad that Brittany's husband was the first to die. He had a construction accident while alone in the woods working on his cabin, just as planned during the game.

Ashley was relieved that the rest of the girls never told Brittany his death was not really an accident. She felt it was a terrible coincidence and the Dolphins wanted to protect her from the knowledge that Theresa had murdered him along with the rest of the husbands before her own accidental death.

Ashley felt a tear roll down the side of her face. "Arrg...Theresa, you are not going to ruin this special day for me. I don't know why I keep letting thoughts of what you did to all of us continuously creep into my mind!" whispered Ashley in stern tone.

She actually wanted to scream it out into the room, but, unfortunately, she was still staying in Theresa's home with Mark and Theresa's three children, Isha, Trystan and Lexi. She wanted to help Mark with his three kids who had just lost their mother. After all, he was kind enough to take her in to live with them for a while after Michael died.

That was one of the hardest things Ashley had ever faced. Staying in the same house with the murderer and not letting Mark know he was next on Theresa's list.

Oh, how the other Dolphins had begged Ashley to stay away from Theresa and not take them up on the offer. At that point in time Ashley was unaware of her pregnancy and felt she had nothing to live for. She believed it was her duty to protect Mark and the rest of her friends from Theresa by knowing Theresa's every move. She had no way of knowing how short her sacrifice would be. The very day she suspected she was pregnant was the day Theresa had her deadly accident.

Ashley climbed out of bed and went to the bathroom to freshen up before joining the rest of the household for breakfast. She ran a brush quickly through her short blond hair. Just as in high school her hair always did exactly what Ashley wanted it to do. She was spared hours of working on it and the cost of perms or color changes.

She threw cold water on her face to try to reduce the swelling that had begun with the tears. She looked carefully at her big brown eyes and smiled at herself in the mirror.

"Today, Mommy, you are going to learn more about your baby," she whispered with excitement.

She went back to her bedroom to dress wondering how much longer her clothes would fit.

"Maybe the time has come to begin some maternity shopping. If everything goes well today with the doctor I'll take Isha and Lexi with me and we can shop for a new wardrobe for baby and me," she whispered.

When Ashley stepped into the kitchen she was surprised to see everyone around the table. Fresh flowers stood tall in a crystal vase placed at the center of the table. Isha and Lexi had the nicest lace tablecloth they owned on the table, and the best dishes. Mark was finishing up the last touches of his quiche presentation and Trystan was pouring the juice into wine glasses.

"What's all of this?" asked Ashley with a sparkle in her voice.

"Your chair, Madame," said Trystan as he pulled out a chair for Ashley.

Mark approached the table with a huge smile on his face. He served the first slice of his famous spinach quiche to Ashley.

"The kids and I felt that the mood in this house has been way too somber for a mommy-to-be and her new baby. It's very hard on all of us losing Theresa, but also unfair to not be sharing in your happy times with you. So from this day forward, we will not impose any more of our sadness on you. We are dedicating ourselves to the joy and celebration of your new baby," announced Mark.

Ashley was touched. She reached out and touched Mark's hand as he started to pull it away from serving her. He paused his movement and let her hand touch his.

She smiled at all of the kids and said, "You guys, you're all so special to me. Thank you for making this special day even more special. I'm not sure I could handle all of this baby stuff alone."

Tears ran down Ashley's face as she looked at her quiche.

Lexi noticed the tears and asked, "What's wrong? Did we do something wrong? Don't you like quiche? We can fix something else if you want."

Mark walked to Lexi's chair and put his hand on her shoulder saying, "Lexi, honey, those are tears of happiness. When you're a grown up woman you'll understand all about crying when you're happy."

"Guess I'm glad I'm a guy," said Trystan stuffing quiche into his mouth.

"Besides everyone knows a pregnant woman is always on the verge of tears. I read that in a magazine somewhere. Right, Ashley?" remarked Isha with an authoritative tone to her voice.

"Right," replied Ashley smiling at Isha.

The remainder of the breakfast conversation turned to chatter about the baby. Will it be a boy or a girl? What names should they consider? What would be the baby-sitting schedule? Who would get to hold it first? Ashley and Mark just sat back, grinning at each other while they watched and listened to the kids making all the plans as if Ashley had nothing to say about them.

7

Then the subject came up about whose room the baby would be sleeping in.

Ashley finally had to butt in, "You know it's really been great of all of you to let me stay here as long as you have, but this house is really not big enough for all of us and a new baby. Your dad's been sleeping on the sofa so I can have his room."

Before she could finish Lexi said, "You know if you and my dad get married then he won't have to sleep on the sofa anymore."

"Lexi!" scolded Mark as his face began to blush.

He glanced at Ashley with a smile and a twinkle in his eye, as if to apologize for his daughter's comment.

Much to his surprise, Ashley's face was glowing bright red. She was cursed with the kind of skin that cannot hide even the slightest hint of embarrassment and she knew it. The color continued to deepen once she knew she had been discovered.

Ashley cleared her throat and continued where she left off, "Actually, I was thinking along a different line of thought. Remember before your mom died we all decided to move into my home here in Denver? It's much larger than this one. I've decided to not sell my other house in New York so we can use it whenever we want. Anyway, I'd like very much if you and your father would consider sharing my home here and helping me to raise the baby. I'll understand if you should choose not to leave here, but

8

the time has come for me to move back and begin work on a nursery for the baby."

Still blushing Ashley looked first at Mark to study his face and then to the children.

Mark looked at his kids and said, "This is a decision that I'm going to leave to the three of you. If you'd like to leave here and move in with Ashley, I'll go along with that plan. If you should choose to stay here I'll understand that as well. We could still visit Ashley as often as you like and help out when the baby comes."

Mark got up and walked to Ashley's chair to pull it out for her. "We're going to give you the privacy you need to discuss this while we go to the livingroom. Oh and as long as you three are stuck in the kitchen, clean it," chuckled Mark as he escorted Ashley out of the kitchen.

Isha threw a dishtowel at him as he walked away.

Ashley sat on the sofa and Mark sat next to her so they could talk without the kids listening.

"What do you think they'll decide?" questioned Ashley.

"Boy, Ash, that's a tough one. This has been the only home they have ever known. I can see it going either way. I'm sure they'd love the extra space when they have friends over not to mention the privacy a larger house has to offer. I can see them not wanting to leave Theresa's presence in this house.

"What about you? Will you miss Theresa's presence?" Ashley quizzed Mark.

As soon as the question left Ashley's mouth she regretted asking Mark such a personal question. Of course he had pleasant memories of Theresa, she was his wife for fifteen years. How could she be so insensitive? He had no idea of the pain and heartache that Theresa caused. He had no idea that he was married to a cold-hearted murderer. He had no idea that he was her next intended victim.

Before Mark had a chance to respond Ashley said, "I'm sorry. I had no right to ask such a question. What I really meant to say is, are you sure you could leave your home of fifteen years and all of the memories?"

"Gosh, I don't know. I guess if it was what the kids wanted I wouldn't deny them the move. I mean it's not like I'm going to rush out and sell this house. The move is only a temporary one to help you through the pregnancy and the birth of the baby and all that goes with it. Once you become an old pro at motherhood you may decide it's time for us to get out from underfoot. Besides, you may meet the love of your life, and then how do you explain a ready made family at home?" answered Mark, all the while trying to find a hint of what Ashley wanted.

In the kitchen Trystan was clearing the table, Lexi was rinsing the dishes and Isha carefully loaded the dishwasher trying to be sure to find enough space for everything to fit in just one load. The house rule was anything that could not fit in the dishwasher had to be hand washed and dried and returned to the cabinet, not

10

left in the sink for the next load of dishes. Trystan and Lexi thought Isha loaded the dishwasher the best, so there was no arguing about her not clearing the table or rinsing.

The sound of dishes and silverware clanging was the only thing that broke the silence of the small kitchen. No one wanted to be the first to start the conversation. Isha and Trystan were both old enough to know that the subject needed to be approached with a little planning, for fear the vote would go two against one. Lexi was more easily persuaded to go along with someone's idea rather than bold enough to stand up for her own. So, whoever won Lexi over had the winning vote.

Lexi broke the silence with, "So are we moving or not?"

"That depends," replied Isha. "How do you feel about moving?"

"Yeah, Lex, what's your vote?" Trystan jumped in.

"I think Daddy and Ashley should get married and then we should all move in together," answered Lexi in a very innocent manner.

"Marriage is a big step," said Isha, "I'm not sure either of them are ready for that right now."

"So if they were ready and wanted to get married, how would you feel about that?" Trystan asked Isha.

"Oh, I don't know. I guess I like Ashley and all, but what if they got married and then decided to move back to New York? I mean that could be exciting and all but I'm not sure I'd want to live there and I'd miss all of my friends," admitted Isha sadly.

"I don't want to move to New York," cried Lexi. "Now I hope they don't get married."

"That's jumping way ahead you guys," Trystan chimed in. "All we are supposed to decide today is whether or not to move out of this house and in with Ashley. Even if we stayed here they could still decide to get married, there is nothing we can do about that. My vote is let's move."

"Trystan's right," agreed Isha. "If they decide to get married it doesn't matter where we're living, and I, for one, would sure like to live in that big house. It's like a mansion. All of my friends would be green with envy. I second the vote to move."

"I like the idea of having a swimming pool in the backyard. I can't wait to have a pool party with all my friends. So I vote yes, too," agreed Lexi.

"Say Mark, while we are alone for a few minutes, I wanted to ask you if it was okay if the girls came along with us today when we go to the doctor for the ultrasound. I thought it would be fun to take them shopping afterward for baby things and a maternity wardrobe for me when I'm fat. That is, if it's okay with you?" asked Ashley shyly. She had never asked anything of Mark since the day she moved in with them.

"Sure, you can take the girls shopping with you. I think they would love it and the ultrasound would be exciting for them. But, I'm not planning to go with you today. I have things to do with my students. I guess I didn't know you wanted me to go. Sorry," responded Mark.

Ashley blushed again. "Oh, I just thought you were planning to go along. I guess it never occurred to me to invite you. I mean I thought you'd want to be there. Oh gosh, I don't know what I thought."

"You look disappointed. I really can't get out of my plans for today," responded Mark. "Can you reschedule your appointment?

"No that's okay. I'm a big girl; I can handle this. Besides, I'm not sure I can wait another day wondering how my baby is doing and if all went well with the invitro process," said Ashley, trying not to show her disappointment. "This'll just be a girl's day out."

The kids came bouncing into the livingroom. Not a moment too soon, thought Ashley hoping to avoid any more of the conversation she and Mark were having.

"Well, what's the verdict?" asked Mark.

"Guess," demanded Lexi.

Mark looked at Lexi; she had that devilish look in her dark eyes as she tossed her black wavy hair over her shoulders. So often he was reminded of Theresa when he looked at her.

"My psychic mind tells me you want to make the move," Mark laughed.

"Wow, how do you do that?" quizzed Lexi.

13

Ashley looked from one child to the next and then to Mark.

"Well, Dad, are we moving?" she asked Mark.

"Guess so," replied Mark.

"Great!" exploded Trystan, "I'll start packing." With that he ran out of the room and up the stairs to his bedroom.

The girls turned to follow him when Mark stopped them.

"Girls, Ashley wants to know if you wanna go with her to the clinic for her ultrasound and then go shopping to start buying baby stuff and clothes for her fat belly. You know, all that yucky girl stuff," teased Mark.

Ashley popped him in the belly, "Big belly huh? Look who's getting a big belly and there's no baby to use for an excuse," joked Ashley.

The girls were thrilled.

"Are you kidding? Of course we want to go!" exclaimed Isha for both of them.

"Well, then, go get ready. I think Ashley wants to leave soon," said Mark while glancing at Ashley for confirmation.

"Yep, I need to leave here in about thirty minutes, that is if I can get my fat belly out the door," she laughed teasingly.

The girls ran to get ready.

"I should head out. Sorry I'm gonna miss out. Maybe I can go to another appointment with you. I really didn't know it meant so much to you. Theresa never liked to have me go along. I think she wanted all of the attention for herself and didn't like it when congratulations and teasing went to me. See ya tonight. Maybe you can tell us if it's Junior or Junette," joked Mark trying to lighten the mood as he headed out the door.

Ashley went back upstairs to change. She had barely begun putting her makeup on when both girls showed up to watch. Isha studied very closely how Ashley used her makeup. At fourteen, make up and hair are everything to girls like Isha. She did not have the same striking dark features as her sister. She favored Mark's green eyes and sandy brown hair. Then, of course, there were the freckles that were impossible to hide.

"Boy you sure put a lot of stuff on your face," said Lexi impatiently. "My mom almost never used makeup."

"Shhh...," scolded Isha. "Dad says not to talk about Mom in front of Ashley," she whispered in Lexi's ear.

"What?" questioned Ashley, as she saw the girls in the mirror, whispering.

"Nothing," said Isha, quickly changing the subject. "You are so lucky you never had freckles to cover up."

Ashley laughed, "I remember feeling the same way about my freckles as you do but they'll fade as you get older. I have to look very hard to find a trace of them now."

She touched her powder to Isha's nose and reminded them it was time to go.

The three of them climbed into the car and fastened their seatbelts. They were only a few blocks from home when Lexi remembered she had to go to the bathroom. Isha was furious with her but Ashley defused the argument by saying, "Good idea, I need to go too. That's what happens when you're pregnant."

Ashley pulled over to a convenience store and they all ran in to use the bathroom. Ashley couldn't resist the craving for ice cream, so she grabbed three ice cream bars.

Isha came up behind her, "Hey, it's morning and we just ate a huge breakfast."

Lexi joined them, "Boy, I'm sure glad you're pregnant, this can be fun," she admitted while ripping the wrapper from her ice cream.

Finally, they arrived at the clinic. Ashley filled out the endless pages of necessary paperwork. Isha thumbed through some magazines about pregnant women and Lexi checked out the kid's books.

Ashley looked around the room at the other women. They looked so tired. Some of them looked so huge, she didn't understand how their stomachs could stretch so far and not burst.

She returned her paperwork to the receptionist and tried to wait patiently for her turn. The office was beautifully decorated with soothing seafoam green wallpaper with soft antique white trim. The carpet swirled various shades of green and the antique white into a calming pattern. Ashley noticed how relaxing the colors were and wondered how to use them in her nursery.

Now she caught herself wondering again if it was a boy or a girl. I guess these colors could work either way. She thought she would give the baby her old room since it was the brightest of the upstairs bedrooms, the only one lacking the heavy dark wood that flowed throughout the house. How she had to beg her mom to change the dark wood to white. Ashley pictured a crib below the window. Her doll collection would be just perfect if she has a little girl. She crossed her fingers hoping for a little girl. She was so focused on the baby lying in her crib in her newly decorated green room that she did not hear the nurse call her name.

Isha nudged her and broke her daydream. Ashley looked at Isha and then heard the nurse repeat her name. Ashley motioned to Lexi to follow them, and they were scooted off to get weighed in and then off to an exam room.

"Remind me not to eat on the way to every doctor visit," laughed Ashley nervously.

She did not have a plan prepared for bad news. Maybe it wasn't a good idea to bring the kids to the first official visit. Once again, her thoughts drifted off to Michael, and how she wished he could be with her today. Somehow though she felt his presence and that comforted her.

17

The doctor stepped into the office and introduced himself to Ashley as he shook her hand. She quickly introduced the girls as her friends, to avoid any embarrassing comments about why they were there or if they were her kids, not that she would mind if they were.

Isha and Lexi fidgeted as the long list of questions were answered. Ashley had to explain her move from New York, where she had had the procedure done, the death of her husband, why she was in Denver, and why she had waited so long to make her appointment.

Once the doctor had all the necessary background information, he palpated Ashley's belly and took a measurement. He looked back at the girls anxiously waiting and said, "Don't you think it's time Mrs. Moore's baby makes his or her television début? Let's see what we can find. Come a little closer."

Ashley was pleased that he included the girls.

A few moments after the doctor applied the gel to Ashley's abdomen, he pressed the probe in a circular motion to find the baby. The girls and Ashley had their eyes glued to the screen.

"See that? Right there," the doctor pointed. "See that pulsating spot there? That's the baby's heart."

Ashley felt a tear roll down her face once again. Oh, Michael, there's your baby, she thought.

"And here's the spine, looks sort of like a string of pearls. Let's get a better look at the head over here...," the doctor paused.

18

Ashley quickly looked from the monitor to the doctor. She saw concern in his face. He had stopped talking and looked deeper into the monitor. He made a couple of adjustments and before he could say a word Lexi popped up with, "Why does the baby have two hearts?"

Ashley quickly turned back to the monitor.

The doctor laughed.

Ashley felt a huge sense of relief that the doctor could laugh at Lexi.

"The baby doesn't have two hearts dear," said the doctor to Lexi, "the mother has two babies."

"Twins!" exploded Isha. "We're gonna have twins!"

Both girls began to jump up and down around the room.

"Are you sure? Are you absolutely sure?" questioned Ashley.

"Yes, Mrs. Moore, you are carrying twins. You should've already been told that could happen when they transferred three embryos into your uterus. Multiple births are very common for invitro fertilization. But everything seems fine. You'll need to come back to see me in one month. Do you have any questions?" he asked as he wiped the gel from Ashley and turned off the machine.

"No, no questions," replied Ashley, still stunned.

Chapter 2

Her nanny, Melissa, tiptoed into the room where Ashley was working on her book.

"They're finally asleep. I think I'll take my break now and be back in an hour. Would you like me to bring something to you before I leave?" asked Melissa as she gathered a clump of loose black curls back into place. The morning had been a tough one with the twins.

Before Ashley could answer, the phone rang and they both dived for it hoping to get to it before it awakened the sleeping babes.

"Hello," whispered Ashley breathlessly.

"Hi, Ash," replied the voice from the phone. It was Susan, one of the Dolphins. Susan was the psychiatrist friend of Ashley's who tried to hold the group together after all the murders. Susan was the brain of the bunch, or so they called her. She was plainer than the other girls, with her dishwater blond hair and hazel eyes. She was not into fashion, or makeup, or the latest hairstyles. She managed to keep her wardrobe filled with strong classics, and wore her hair pulled up to maintain her professional image. Susan's husband, Brian, was the second murdered husband.

"Hi Susan, we just got the twins to sleep. Melissa and I have been trying to comfort them all morning. They share everything including this nasty cold that is going around. I think the older kids bring home every germ known to man. Schools are a breeding ground for germs I'm convinced. What's up?" asked Ashley.

"Stop me if you disagree but December is approaching and it will be five years since *that* slumber party. I think enough time has gone by that it would be good for all of us to get together again and see how the healing process has gone. What do you think? I mean, we can't avoid seeing each other forever. I think we should face our fears and meet again." Susan paused. "You're not stopping me, does that mean you agree?"

"I'm not sure, give me some time to think about it. Everything is going so well now. We had some pretty rough times in the beginning. The kids hated their new schools and had some difficulty making friends. They were not as thrilled as we had hoped when Mark and I decided to get married a year ago. The twins have been a handful, but now with my nanny Melissa helping I can get back to my writing. My agent has been so patient. I guess maybe I'm afraid to feel those feelings again. I'm afraid..., what can I say, I'm just afraid," sighed Ashley.

"My point exactly. I think we are all somewhat afraid. Once we get together and have a great time and part ways and nothing happens, I feel we can put it to rest once and for all," pleaded Susan.

"Hmm...I suppose now that Theresa is no longer with us the reunion could actually be fun if we tried to make the past go away. If the others agree, count me in," said Ashley reluctantly.

"I have one more favor to ask of you," begged Susan.

"I'm feeling in a generous mood, shoot," replied Ashley.

"I think we should meet at the scene of our pain. I think we should all get together again at your house. We don't have to stay with you. We can stay at motels, but we could plan a meal or something," said Susan.

"Whoa, return to the scene of the crime. That's a tough one. But you know I've redone the house over the last few years and it feels like the energy here has improved. Maybe it would help everyone feel better. Okay, you're on but you'll have to connect with everyone. I'll supply the food and the house," agreed Ashley.

Ashley hung up the phone and a chill went down her spine. She walked back to her desk and sat down at her computer. Her hands felt cold as she tried to type. She sat back in her chair and rubbed her eyes. She had lost all focus for her writing. Her thoughts kept drifting back to the slumber party. She had to make this party so

22

different from the first. It would be fun to see everyone again and to share stories of all of the new babies. She was very anxious to show off Arianna and Nathan, her twins. That's it, she thought, we'll make this get-together a happy time for all the kids. We'll turn it into a big Christmas party. She felt her fear of the party fade and be replaced with a warm happy feeling. Maybe Susan was right after all.

That evening when Mark and the kids came home, she tossed the idea out at them. Trystan said he would help. Lexi wanted to know if presents would be involved. Mark said he would've liked to help with the food, but he would be too busy. Isha was away at college, but she did love a good party.

After Mark moved his family in with Ashley he felt somewhat like a freeloader. His income from teaching music at the university was not nearly enough to raise his kids, the twins and support Ashley, not to mention the upkeep on the house. Ashley tried to convince him she had enough money for all of them but Mark was too proud to accept that.

Ashley's late husband Michael had made a connection for Mark at his recording company in New York. Mark called the contact person and set up an appointment to meet with him. The meeting was magical and Mark was well on his way to fame and fortune. The only problem being he was overwhelmed with work, just like Michael had been. He had almost no time for Ashley and the kids. What little time he did have, he tried to give to his own kids. Ashley tried to understand, but frequently found herself feeling hurt and left out. She was happy for Mark's success, but really liked it better when he was around more.

While Theresa was alive she pressured Mark constantly to improve himself and not to settle for his small income. She thought he was capable of bigger and better accomplishments. She was raised in the lap of luxury and her marriage to Mark was more like the lake of poverty. She hated being poor. After Theresa died Mark became everything Theresa had begged for. He became financially successful, living in a huge home and traveling wherever and whenever he wanted. His kids became well provided for and quickly learned to live the rich life style and enjoy it tremendously.

In early November, Ashley heard from Susan again. She managed to convince everyone to come except for Brittany. After the slumber party and all the deaths, Brittany was far too fragile to relive the past. She told Susan she had no intention of putting herself or her kids through that kind of pain again. It was probably just as well because, now the others could talk freely about Theresa and the murders that they hid from Brittany.

Amy, a criminal attorney, moved to Denver to practice law after the death of her husband Jonathon. She remained a man hater, and never remarried. He was victim number three. Amy had no kids of her own and was grateful that Jonathon's wild and insensitive boys were out of her life forever. She poured herself into her career and created quite a name for herself among her colleagues.

Amy and Ashley would get together occasionally. Mark was always suggesting a blind date for Amy, but she wouldn't hear of it. Mark thought that was such a waste. She had so much to offer. She was absolutely beautiful with her shiny dark brown shoulder length hair, dark eyes, and deep wine colored lips against a perfect complexion. Not to mention her perfect body and grace. She would have been any man's dream, beauty, brains and money.

Ashley knew she could count on Amy to help her with the party arrangements now that Susan had talked Amy into attending the party.

Finally there would be Stephanie, red haired and loud in a socially acceptable sort of way. Stephanie owned her own ad agency in Los Angeles. She was tall and thin. Her presence was known the moment she entered a room. She had a strong passion for food, especially sweets and even more so the chocolate variety.

Stephanie's husband Richard had been the fourth husband to die. Before his death he and Stephanie had created frozen embryos that were stored at a frozen embryo bank. Shortly after his death Stephanie had an embryo transplanted and gave birth to her oldest son

Kent. A year later she repeated the procedure and had another son, Tom.

Ashley was very anxious to see Stephanie and her boys. The party would not be the same without this fiery redhead.

The party was on and Ashley began her plans. She called a caterer and put Trystan and a few of his friends to work decorating anything that didn't move. Money was no object; she wanted her house and property to look like a winter wonderland.

The party was set for the first weekend in December. The boys worked hard on the decorations. Ashley was impressed. Lexi was so excited about everything. Ashley liked to watch the look in the eyes of her three-year-old twins as the decorations took shape.

When Isha came home for Thanksgiving Ashley whisked her away to go shopping for three days. She wanted gifts for everyone. Isha suggested she hire a Santa for the kids and Ashley loved the idea so that was added to her list.

Mark walked into the house on Sunday night to see what looked like an entire store of packages spilling out from room to room.

"This is some Christmas party you're planning, Ash, teased Mark. "Do you think one weekend is enough to open all of these gifts?"

"Well hello, stranger," squealed Ashley as she jumped into Mark's arms.

Mark held her while they kissed a long passionate kiss. Their time together was so precious. Ashley stopped her work on the packages to be with Mark. She poured out all of the details of the party to him, including the Santa idea.

"You know I haven't received an invitation yet," joked Mark.

"I told you this is just a girls' and kids' party remember?" responded Ashley.

"I know, I know, but I thought since there was going to be a man here in a red suit one more man might not matter," teased Mark.

"This is your home, so if you want to hang around I guess it'd be okay," replied Ashley, wondering if he really wanted to be there.

"I'll probably just pop in once in awhile to see if you need anything, but other than that I'll stay out of your hair. That's the beauty of such a big house. I can lurk anywhere and no one would even notice me," said Mark.

The final plans were made for the party. The guests would arrive with their kids in time for lunch. There would be songs, gifts, and games for all. Ashley and Melissa had prepared a playroom for all the kids and Melissa arranged for some of her friends to help with the nanny duties for the extra children. That would allow the adults some quiet time in the evening for their own party.

It was the night before the big party. Trystan was rushing around to check all the lights and animations to be sure they were in working order. Mark carried down an old overstuffed chair from the attic that would be perfect near the tree for the kids to greet and talk with Santa.

Trystan found an old Christmas decoration of Rudolph in the attic while helping Mark with the chair. "Hey, check this out. I think I can use this," said Trystan excitedly.

"Wait, that wire looks too frayed to be safe," Mark pointed out.

"That's okay, I'll just rewire it," replied Trystan.

Trystan headed to the basement. Mark turned the entire basement into an outstanding workshop. Ashley, like Theresa before her, never ventured into Mark's workspace in the basement but for an entirely different reason. Theresa did not like to see Mark's junk, as she called it. Ashley on the other hand still stayed clear of the basement because her father had fallen down the basement steps to his death when she was a child. To this day she still didn't know if he fell accidentally or if her mother pushed him in a drunken rage while she was throwing him out that night after learning about his affair with Amy's mother.

Trystan was checking out Mark's endless supply of electrical wiring when he noticed a wire along the ceiling joists running the length of the board above Mark's desk and into a recording system. Trystan, curious now, followed the other end of the wire. He traced it to under the livingroom where it spliced off to the den. As he

28

followed the wire from under one room to the next he realized that the wiring went to each room of the first level of the house. Strange, he thought. Why would dad have the house bugged? He was willing to bet that the second level where the bedrooms were probably had the same wiring system.

"Can I help with your Rudolph light?" questioned Mark.

The sound of his dad's voice behind him made Trystan nearly jump out of his skin.

"What's wrong" asked Mark, "are you having trouble finding what you need?"

"Uh, no," replied Trystan, "I was just curious. What are these wires for? Is this house bugged?"

Mark looked concerned and then made the quick comment, "Oh those wires, I put those in just before the twins were born. I wanted to be able to hear them if they woke up while Ashley was out and I was caring for them. I could work in my shop and not miss a peep out of them no matter which room they were in."

"Wouldn't it have been easier to just use the baby monitor?" asked Trystan.

"I suppose so, but I was worried about getting all the way down here to realize I forgot to bring the monitor with me or the kids might be in two separate rooms or they would be in a room that didn't have a base unit in it. This way I could track them from here at any time."

"Are you telling me you have my room bugged too?" demanded Trystan in an angry voice.

"I guess so. I've never had the twins in your room so I've never had reason to listen in. Why is there something you are hiding from me?" questioned Mark trying to shift the accusations that were mounting.

"No, nothing," scowled Trystan as he left the room to head back upstairs, no longer interested in his latest treasure to be repaired.

Trystan headed immediately to his room and searched for the wiring that bugged his room. He moved every piece of furniture until he found it. When he did he disconnected the wire.

"There," he mumbled softly to himself, "now Dad will never know I cut the wires unless he is really trying to bug my room."

Trystan spent the rest of the evening in his room. There was a knock at his door and in popped Isha.

"Hey, what's up? You did a great job with the decorations. Ashley went all out this year. Sounds like a great party tomorrow. Hope I don't get stuck with the brats," Isha remarked.

"Not a chance. Ashley has three nannies hired for the day," stated Trystan.

"Oh, the joy of money. Sure glad we have it now. Remember how it used to be when Mom was alive?" reminded Isha.

"Yeah, I guess now I understand more about how angry she was to be poor," admitted Trystan.

Trystan jumped off of his bed and went to the door. He popped his head out and peered both ways down the long hall. No one was there. He turned to Isha and said, "Dad has this house bugged. He gave me some lame excuse about wanting to hear the twins wherever they were, but I don't buy it. So be warned your room is probably bugged as well. I disconnected mine."

"What!" exclaimed Isha. "Don't tell me he listens to my phone calls. That is like a major invasion of my privacy. How dare he? Are you sure? That doesn't sound like Dad."

"Okay I'll prove it, let's go to your room," insisted Trystan.

Isha and Trystan walked down the hall to Isha's room.

"Does that mean Dad has the guest rooms bugged too? He can listen to everything Ashley's friends will be talking about. That sure seems kinda creepy," Isha commented as they walked past the guest rooms.

Once inside the room Isha stood watch at the door and Trystan searched Isha's room.

"Here it is. What did I tell you? Dad's had us bugged," Trystan reported.

Isha walked over to the spot on the floor where the wire came into her room.

31

"This is new, Trystan. This wasn't here when I was home for Thanksgiving. I dropped my ring and it rolled under the desk right here where the wire comes in. I pulled the desk away from the wall to look for my ring. I would've seen this wire and might even have disconnected it by pulling the desk out. No, I know this wasn't here a few weeks ago," insisted Isha.

"Well if you are so sure it wasn't here a few weeks ago then why is Dad bugging the house now? The twins are old enough to go look for him and call him if they need him. He lied to me," remarked Trystan.

"The party, that's it! Dad wants to bug the party that Ashley's having, but why? What could a bunch of old school friends have to talk about that would be of any interest to Dad? I mean, all they're gonna talk about is their kids and stuff like that," Isha said.

"Since Dad has it hooked up to his recording system, I'll make sure to find the time while he's gone to search his workshop for the tape to see what's on it," Trystan confided.

"Well Sherlock, I'm glad you're on the job, but I'm tired and would like to get some sleep before our house fills up tomorrow and we can't find a peaceful spot in it," yawned Isha as she pushed Trystan out into the hall.

The sun was barely up in Isha's room when she felt the movement of her bedding all around her. She woke knowing someone was crawling into bed with her. It took her a moment to realize she was home and not at the dorm. She opened her eyes. Lexi, Arianna, and Nathan were all sitting on her bed looking at her.

They were asleep when Isha came home the night before. Now they were anxious to see her and tell her all about the party. Isha pretended she knew nothing of the party and that added to their excitement to tell her more.

She got up and shooed them out of her room as she followed them to the hall and down the stairs to the kitchen for breakfast.

Trystan left for the day, coward that he was. Ashley was off to the airport to pick up Stephanie and her boys. Mark was downstairs in his shop and Melissa was cleaning up the breakfast dishes from the kids.

"Good morning Melissa," yawned Isha.

"Good morning," grunted Melissa rudely as she left the kitchen. She didn't care much for Isha or Trystan. She even treated Lexi badly when no one was around. She only liked the twins and felt Mark neglected Ashley and the twins while he spoiled the older kids. She resented them for that. She really thought Mark was slipping with his duties as a father figure for the twins.

At the airport, Ashley nervously awaited Stephanie's flight. It had been postponed due to bad weather conditions in Los Angeles. Ashley hoped that Stephanie was on the flight and had not changed her mind.

She paced anxiously back and forth in front of the board that posted the flights. The plane was scheduled to arrive any minute.

The plane landed and the passengers began to unload. Before Ashley could see Stephanie she could hear her. Ashley was waiting near the luggage area. Stephanie appeared chasing two small children. Ashley laughed. Kent, her three- year- old, had a full head of dark curly hair. Tom, the two-year-old, had his mother's flaming red hair and the energy that goes with it.

Stephanie looked up and saw Ashley, she screamed to her, "Don't just stand there, grab the redhead and don't let go."

Ashley reached out and snatched the leash that was attached to a harness on Tom. He had been cooped up on the plane just a little too long. Ashley gathered him up into her arms and headed towards Stephanie. She gave Stephanie a big hug while Kent ran circles around them tangling them with his leash.

"I'll never travel alone with these two again unless they are tranquilized. I sure hope you have something great to eat at your house I'm starved and exhausted," moaned Stephanie.

Ashley helped Stephanie with her luggage and the two boys as they walked to her car. Thank goodness she had twins so there were already two carseats secured in her backseat. Once the boys were strapped in they were off to Ashley's house with Stephanie talking a mile a minute all the way. It wasn't difficult to figure out where her boys got all their energy.

The doorbell rang. Isha waited for Melissa to get it, but of course she didn't. She was the nanny not the maid she kept reminding everyone. The doorbell rang again. Isha had hoped Lexi or one of the twins would get it. Finally, the third time it rang, Isha went off to answer it.

"Hi Isha, remember me? I'm Susan and this is Megan and Dawn."

"Sure, I remember you. You spent the night with us once. Your husband died at the motel." Immediately Isha wanted to take back her last sentence. "I mean sure, how have you been? Come in. Let me take your coats," Isha responded with embarrassment covering her face.

Susan and the girls stepped into the family room. There was a fire in the fireplace. Susan stopped for a moment to admire it. She remembered the night of the slumber party. The power had gone out and they went out in the storm to bring in firewood to start a fire for warmth that night. How different this fire was, so much warmer and brighter. The flames danced happily instead of the reflections of sadness from that night.

Mark suddenly appeared from nowhere.

"I thought I heard voices," commented Mark. "Susan it's so good to see you and who are these two beautiful ladies you have with you?"

Susan quickly introduced the girls.

35

Megan was adopted when Brian was still alive. She was sweet sixteen and not too thrilled to be at this ridiculous reunion. Dawn was the baby that was conceived the morning of the day that Brian was killed at the Adams Mark Hotel.

Dawn was three years old, the same age as the twins. She had been looking forward to the party.

Isha disappeared from the room leaving Mark to tend to the guests until Ashley returned.

Isha wondered if Mark had been listening to the house to know Susan had arrived. How else would he have heard voices from the basement? The house is much too large and soundproof for that. She wondered if she could slip downstairs unnoticed to see if the recorder was on.

She glanced at her Dad busy visiting with Susan and made a run for it. She went directly to Mark's desk and tried to figure out the volume control for the tape recorder that appeared to running at the moment. Suddenly from behind a hand reached out and covered her mouth. Isha wanted to scream but couldn't. She struggled, kicking and striking out at her assailant. She heard Trystan's giggle and then his hand released from her mouth.

Isha turned to Trystan and punched him in the stomach.

"Hey, what'd ya do that for?" asked Trystan breathlessly.

36

"Why did you scare me and what are you doing here anyway, I thought you were gone for the day?" quizzed Isha still angry and shaking from Trystan's little joke.

"Shhh...I decided to spy on Dad," explained Trystan. "I thought it would be fun. There are so many places to hide down here. By the way, he was listening to the living room. He knew it was Susan before he even went upstairs. He flipped the switch to turn it on when he heard the doorbell ring."

Just then they heard Ashley walk in with Stephanie. They listened for a moment and then decided to disappear again before Mark returned. Isha went back to her room and Trystan melted into the dark shadows of the basement.

Chapter 3

Stephanie, Ashley and the two boys entered the house with much commotion. This was normal for Stephanie, but a bit exhausting for Ashley. She had no idea how easy the twins were until she spent the last hour with Stephanie and her boys.

The weather for December was unseasonably warm, quite a change from the blizzard conditions of the past party. Susan stepped out from the family room to greet Stephanie and Ashley.

"I'm glad you could come," whispered Susan as she gave Stephanie a big hug.

"It's great to see you again," admitted Ashley as she and Susan hugged.

"Wow! Things look different around here," exclaimed Stephanie as she started to snoop around. "This doesn't look like the same place. I mean I thought when we pulled up out front the decorations made everything look so new and different but you've made

38

some monstrous changes in here. It's so bright and cheery. Much, much better, good work Ash."

"Isn't it wonderful? I had Mark give me the grand tour. I love it. He took my bags from the car and moved me into one of your guest rooms. Really Ashley, I thought we were going to be staying at hotels," commented Susan.

"Nope, why bother when we have so much space here? This will be cozier. It made the most sense for everyone to stay here," replied Ashley.

"Sounds perfect to me," agreed Stephanie, "I'm not ready for another car trip with these guys anytime soon."

Stephanie pointed to the boys but they were already gone.

"Now, where did they go?" scowled Stephanie as she took off towards the stairs to find them. She met Melissa on the stairs with Tom and Kent.

"Are you missing these two?" she quizzed.

"I'm so sorry, I let go of them for just a moment and they were gone," apologized Stephanie.

Melissa responded, "Not a problem, Miss, I'll just take them to the toy room to play with the other children."

Stephanie sighed a sigh of relief as Melissa and the boys headed toward the toy room.

Ashley and Susan were already in the kitchen getting lunch ready for Stephanie. They were sure her first words when she stepped into the kitchen would be about food.

Stephanie opened the door to the kitchen and demanded, "Where's the food?"

Everyone laughed. The party was on.

Trystan and Isha made an appearance in the kitchen to see when lunch would be ready. Megan followed them closely.

Isha felt sorry for Megan being dragged along to this reunion with her mom and a house full of little kids so she befriended her. Once Isha introduced Megan to Trystan it was love at first sight for Megan. Trystan was very mature for a seventeen-year-old and sixteen-year-old Megan could not take her eyes off of him.

Isha and Megan helped in the kitchen. Trystan carried food to the buffet table in the dining room. Once the food was nearly ready to be served, Ashley wondered where Mark had disappeared to and was about to go to look for him when he suddenly appeared in the dining room ready to eat.

"How did you know the food was ready?" questioned Ashley.

"Psychic remember?" teased Mark.

Trystan and Isha shot glances at each other. They knew where he had been and what he had been doing. They were right. Mark was spying on Ashley's party.

Stephanie asked, "Where are the kids? Shouldn't we feed them now?"

"Melissa and her crew will be taking care of that. The kids will be fed and put down for naps. When they

40

wake we'll have their Christmas party and a certain visitor will be here for them. They'll be bathed and put to bed so we can have the day and the evening alone," beamed Ashley. "Unless of course you ladies would prefer to take care of them yourselves. Maybe I should've asked first."

Susan and Stephanie began talking at the same time.

"Good idea," said Stephanie.

"Great planning. A break would be good," agreed Susan.

The older children, Mark, and the ladies had a nice visit during lunch.

"Where's Amy?" asked Stephanie.

"She's planning to come after the kids are asleep," responded Ashley. "Aunt Amy just loves the twins but only in small doses. The extra kids were a bit more than she thought she could handle."

One of the hired girls came to clear the table. Mark disappeared into the vast house again. Isha, Trystan and Megan went for a walk around the grounds.

"Shall we go into the other room for coffee?" suggested Ashley.

Ashley, Susan and Stephanie sat quietly for a few moments.

Susan began, "Well so far, so good. We all made it and Ashley's right, the energy of this house has changed. How have you been dealing with all of this Stephanie?"

"It's getting better. The boys are quite a handful but they are all I have left of Richard. I'm so glad we planned ahead for the babies. Dealing with the fact Richard was murdered was the most difficult thing I've ever had to face. I could never have made it without our boys," sighed Stephanie.

"I've managed to keep the ad agency going for the time being. The boys go to a wonderful day care and seem happy. I just don't know what I plan to tell them when they ask questions about Richard. I guess I will just lie and tell them it was an accident. I mean, what good would it do to tell them Theresa caused the explosion in his firework shed? I plan to tell them it was an accident, just like the police report said. Nothing can be done about it now, and how would they feel knowing I knew his life was in danger and I couldn't stop it from happening?" sobbed Stephanie with tears running down her face.

Ashley handed a tissue to her.

"I'm sorry, I thought I could handle talking about all of this," apologized Stephanie.

"I thought this was supposed to be an up party," whined Amy as she entered the room her arms loaded with packages.

"Amy," called Susan from across the room, "I thought you weren't coming until this evening."

"Changed my mind. The last time you girls got together without me to talk I ended up drugged and driven half way across the country. I still remember the doozy of a headache when the sedatives wore off. I'm here to protect myself from all of you," laughed Amy.

This caused all of the Dolphins to laugh and Stephanie was relieved that Amy walked in when she did.

Amy hugged all of the girls. She sat with Stephanie and asked, "So what did they do to you to make you cry?"

"We were talking about the boys and how I should tell them what happened to Richard," responded Stephanie.

"Hell, you're gonna lie to them aren't you? Why tell them Theresa killed their dad? I, for one, would prefer no one ever had the opportunity to look into any of this mess. I say let the past stay in the past. I've worked too hard on my career to have it damaged by a murder scandal. Theresa has caused enough damage. Let's not let her cause any more from the grave. Why in the hell are you guys drinking coffee like some tea party dames? I need a drink," moaned Amy as she headed to the bar across the room.

The other girls quickly joined her.

"Now that's more like it. We could all use a few drinks to loosen up and face the ghosts of our past," toasted Amy lifting her glass.

Mark stepped into the room to welcome Amy. "Speaking of ghosts," laughed Susan. "Mark just seems to appear and disappear around here. Watch what you say you never know where he could be lurking."

Susan made this comment as both a joke and a warning. They never told Mark what they knew about Theresa. The girls kept their pact to tell no one. They knew only bad things could happen once their secret was out.

Mark flirted a bit with Amy and she gave him a bad time. Their friendship blossomed through Ashley. Amy spent a great deal of time in their home.

Susan asked Mark, "Would you like to join us?"

"Not on your life. I don't think I'd fit in with all the girl talk," commented Mark. "I'm outa here."

Mark walked across the room to Ashley and kissed her good-bye.

"I've got a few errands to run; the house is yours," said Mark.

"Boy does that seem strange, watching Mark kiss you. I keep getting this feeling to duck or something in case Theresa decides to throw something at you," joked Stephanie.

"So how is married life with Mark and all the kids?" questioned Susan.

"Oh, exhausting at times but pretty good," replied Ashley.

"You mean you are married to Mr. Wonderful, the world's greatest husband and all you can say is okay?" teased Stephanie.

"Don't get me wrong, Mark's a great guy, that is, when he's around. Once he got that recording contract and became secure with his business success, I never get to see him. He's either with his students, off recording somewhere, working in the basement or doing something with his kids. It's kinda hard to do much with the twins along. That's one of the reasons I hired Melissa. She's become more than just a nanny. She's become more of my confidant. She knows how lonely I am for Mark."

"Sometimes I think I confide in her too much. She's become cold to Mark and his kids in defense of my feelings and the twins. She is anxious for his kids to grow up and move away. She barely speaks to Isha when she comes home for the holidays."

"Theresa didn't appreciate what she had in Mark. I would much rather have the marriage they had than the busy life Mark has now, especially since we don't need the money," explained Ashley.

"You've never told Mark anything about Theresa have you?" questioned Stephanie.

"No, I couldn't do that to his memory of her. Besides we have a promise to never tell anyone and I plan to keep that promise," responded Ashley.

"What's your life like now, Doc?" asked Amy.

Susan answered, "It's good. I've cut back a little on the number of new patients. I'm trying to find more time for Megan and Dawn. Megan has never accepted Dawn completely. She was devastated when Brian was killed. Then, at a time when she needed me most I was pregnant with Dawn. I was busy at work, sick most mornings and exhausted when Megan would come home from school. I feel I really wasn't there for her. I think she feels less important in my life now that I have a biological daughter of my own. It may have been easier on her if Dawn had been a boy."

"Have you seen a good shrink about this?" teased Stephanie.

Susan tossed a sofa pillow at her spilling her drink on the carpet.

Susan felt badly and set her drink down to clean up the mess she created. While she was bent over the carpet dabbing up the drink she felt another pillow come down hard upon her head. Stephanie had retaliated. Soon Amy and Ashley joined in and they were having one huge pillow fight when the older kids walked in.

Megan looked shocked. She had never seen anything but a totally in control professional side of her mother. Isha just rolled her eyes and laughed. Trystan suggested that maybe they had had too much to drink so early in the day.

Susan sent a pillow flying across the room at Megan. Megan grabbed it and hit Trystan with it. He wrestled her to the ground to tickle her and Isha picked up the pillow and began to beat Trystan off of Megan.

Suddenly a very stern Melissa showed up in the room. She was prepared to scold Isha and Trystan for waking the children with all of the noise. Ashley looked up when she saw Melissa walk in. She was about to speak to her when a pillow came flying past her face and she ducked.

Melissa said, "The children are awake and would like to open their gifts now. What would you like me to tell them?"

Ashley looked at her watch. It was nearly three o'clock. Santa was to arrive at three-thirty.

"Please get them ready to come down then call me when they are ready," suggested Ashley.

Stephanie, looking like a child that got caught doing something wrong, began to gather the pillows and straighten the family room. The others joined in to help.

"I tell you there is something about this house that still brings out the kid in me. I'm sorry," apologized Stephanie.

"No, please don't apologize," begged Ashley, "That's what this party is for. We're here to have fun like we did when we were kids growing up here. We're here to forget the last party and replace the bad memories with new."

Melissa stepped back into the room to announce the children were ready. At that very moment the doorbell rang. Amy went to the door while Ashley and the other mothers went to gather their children.

When the group returned to the room Amy took Ashley aside and said, "You're never going to believe this but you have Santa Claus at your door."

"Oh good, he's here," said Ashley excitedly.

47

Amy looked puzzled but sat down with the rest.

Ashley went to the door to work out the details of Santa's entrance. She joined the others near the tree. The kids were busy shaking gifts and looking at the sparkling ornaments on the tree when suddenly there came a hearty, "Ho, Ho, Ho, Merry Christmas!" as Santa entered the room.

The twins, Nathan and Arianna, began to cry. Dawn ran to her mother for protection. Kent and Tom ran to Santa and began to climb on him. Santa walked across the room and sat on the large overstuffed chair brought down for the occasion.

One by one the children warmed up to the jolly man dressed in red that kept giving them gifts and candy. Trystan, Megan and Isha came in to watch. Trystan started the Christmas music. Ashley served hot cocoa, and eggnog. The party was picture perfect. Mark came in shortly after things were well underway. Once again a remark was made about his impeccable timing.

Even Amy had a good time watching the kids. She sat on Santa's lap herself. Mark teased her about finally finding the right man. The party kept going for three hours.

The excitement, the candy, and need for sleep soon caused the party to come to an end for the kids. Melissa and her crew whisked the kids off to feed them supper and prepare them for bed.

Mark and Trystan cleaned up all of the wrapping paper. Megan snuggled into her mother on the sofa where she could watch Trystan. Susan was pleased to hold Megan closely.

The room was cleared of the paper and bows. The dishes were taken to the kitchen and there was a quiet time in the room. The fire crackled and the Christmas music still played softly in the background. The adults gathered around Santa as he prepared to leave. They thanked him for the great job with the kids. Mark walked him to the door and paid him his fee plus a generous tip.

The women were busily talking about the party and the expressions on the kid's faces. They thanked Ashley over and over again for all of her hard work. She stood up to take a bow. She grabbed Susan, who had the idea for a gathering, and forced her to take a bow.

Mark and the older kids excused themselves from the gushy conversation and disappeared to other parts of the house.

Soon the children were paraded in to say their good nights to their mothers. While the moms were busy talking the kids were fed, bathed and put into their pajamas. Susan wanted to put Dawn to bed herself. Ashley hugged and kissed the twins goodnight. Stephanie blew her boys kisses from across the room and told Melissa they were hers for the night.

The caterer arrived while the Dolphins were talking. Mark had let them in to set up. He called the girls into the dining room. He filled a plate for himself. He suggested to Isha that maybe they should do the same and then leave the friends alone for the evening.

Mark never appeared again that night.

Isha, Trystan and Megan watched movies and ate popcorn the rest of the evening.

The Dolphins spent their time eating, talking, and playing games in true slumber party fashion as the hours ticked by. It was two o'clock in the morning before they decided to call it a night and retreat to bed.

Ashley crawled into bed with Mark.

"Well, how was your party?" questioned Mark.

"Oh, honey, it was the greatest day. Thanks for all the help and everything you did."

"I didn't do anything, Ash, I just stayed out of your way. I'm glad all went well. Did you share secrets all evening the way girls like to do?"

"We don't have any secrets," lied Ashley. "What makes you think we have secrets?"

"Just thought women always have some secrets. That's what keeps them such a mystery to men," yawned Mark as he rolled over to sleep.

Ashley lay awake wondering what Mark had meant or if he had overheard something.

The next morning, one by one, the Dolphins arrived in the kitchen looking for that morning cup of coffee.

"Remember the last party when Theresa had forgotten to buy the coffee?" reminded Stephanie.

"How could I forget?" said Amy. "She could've killed me with that candlestick holder she threw at me."

"Well maybe you shouldn't have called her a bitch," reminded Susan.

"This party was so much better," chimed in Stephanie. "The food was great, the company was great, and the kids had a wonderful time. I would rate this party a ten. I know I'm going to have to drag the boys out of here kicking and screaming."

"I'm not sure Megan is ready to leave either. Have you seen the way she looks at Trystan?" sighed Susan.

"You know you guys are the only real family I have except for Ashley and the twins. I'd really like to do this again sometime," suggested Amy.

"Are we taking a vote on that?" asked Stephanie. "If so my vote is we do this again."

"Well, it's been five years since the last party. What do you say every five years we journey to one of our homes and do it again?" agreed Susan.

"That would be silly. I don't mind having it here. I think now it should become a tradition. Let's do this every five years until we are either too old or too tired of each other. What do ya say?" asked Ashley.

"Does that mean we are not going to see each other again for five years? That's not what I had in mind," moaned Amy.

51

"Of course not," said Susan. "We can get together and visit whenever we want, but we'll just have an official Christmas party here every five years."

The remainder of the morning was a slow sleepy one. The Dolphins were tired from staying up late. Melissa's crew returned that morning to help with the kids.

Trystan, Isha and Megan came down for breakfast together.

"Where's Dad?" asked Trystan.

"He left about an hour ago. He had to meet with a student or something. I forgot he had an appointment until I heard his car leaving the driveway this morning. I looked out the window and saw him drive away."

The older kids excused themselves from the table.

"Come on," said Trystan to Isha.

Isha stopped him and nodded towards Megan who was tagging along.

They headed for the basement workshop. Once they arrived downstairs Trystan suggested, "Hey Megan, have Isha show you all the cool junk Dad has down here."

Isha picked up on the hint and took Megan off to another room in the large basement while Trystan raced to the recording device on Mark's desk.

Mark had set the recorder before he left. The conversations upstairs were being taped again. Trystan was curious about how the system worked. How did his dad know which room to turn on at what time? Then he realized it must be voice activated. He found the stack of tapes Mark had recorded yesterday during the party. They were labeled Christmas party. He was anxious to listen to them to see if he could discover what had intrigued his dad so much that he had to bug the house before the guests arrived.

He heard Megan's voice as she and Isha approached the room where Trystan was snooping. He put the tapes back and thought he would have to find another time to listen to them to discover the mystery.

The group returned to the main level of the house. They barely reached the family room when the front door opened and Mark entered. He waved good morning to everyone on his way to the basement.

Trystan and Isha shared a glance of relief. It was a good thing Megan had tagged along, or they would've been discovered snooping in Mark's private work area.

The weekend party was over. One by one, the guests began to leave. Stephanie and the boys were the last to leave. Ashley drove them to the airport.

After the party, Isha returned to school. Trystan never made the time to listen to the tapes that Mark had recorded. As time past they were forgotten entirely.

Eventually, Trystan moved away to college. Isha met the love of her life; they were married. The tension mounted between Ashley and Mark. Mark became totally absorbed into his music career. He quit his job at the university and spent most of his time in Ashley's New York home.

Melissa was still with them, all the while desperately trying to coax Ashley into divorcing Mark, freeing herself to move on with her life. Isha and her husband moved to New York. Trystan was already attending school there. It was as if their original family regrouped in New York with occasional visits to Lexi, Ashley, and the twins in Denver.

The little time Ashley and Mark spent together was not happy. Most of it was spent arguing about Mark always being gone. Melissa kept the anger going. She used to lecture Mark about what a terrible husband he was. He would threaten to fire her. Ashley wouldn't hear of it, so Melissa knew her job was secure. Melissa wished she could drive Mark and his kids away for good. Then Ashley would have the opportunity to meet a decent man and have a good husband and father for the twins.

The Dolphins kept their promise to each other. Five years later they returned for yet another perfect Christmas party. The kids were growing, causing the house to be more active with excitement. The youngsters were nearly eight years old now. Christmas was much more magical and exciting to them than the last party when they were three.

Ashley insisted Mark and his kids return home for the party. She planned to hide how sour their relationship had turned from her friends. Isha's husband could not get away, so she went home without him.

Trystan was not around this year to help with decorations, so Ashley hired a crew to handle everything. Once again the grounds were beautifully decorated, as was the house. Ashley tried to duplicate the party of five years ago. She begged Amy not to tell Susan and Stephanie about the problems she and Mark were having.

Ashley pulled off another wonderful party. Everyone had a great time. The kids had been looking forward to the party for months.

Later that evening, when the kids were asleep, the Dolphins gathered in the family room. Food and drinks were flowing abundantly. Isha and Trystan filled their plates and disappeared upstairs to Isha's old room. Mark went off to the basement.

"Where's Megan?" asked Ashley.

"She didn't want to come this year," stammered Susan, with her lip quivering.

"Okay, spill it," coaxed Amy. "Heaven knows you can tell us anything."

"She's not doing very well," confided Susan. "She's gotten herself mixed up with drugs. She's in a rehab hospital. I can't even see her. I can't believe I'm a psychiatrist and I let this happen to my own daughter."

Stephanie sat next to Susan and put her arms around her. "How can we help?"

"I wish I knew," cried Susan.

The remainder of the evening was not as joyous as the last party had been. As the wine flowed Ashley felt more comfortable expressing her pain from her failed marriage to Mark.

Stephanie admitted motherhood and work were a little too much for her. She met a wonderful man, but he hated kids. She feared she would spend the rest of her life alone.

Amy was the only one that had good news to share. There was no man in her life; of course, she thought that contributed to her sanity. Her good news was she had recently been appointed judge. She restrained herself from telling Ashley sooner because she wanted to break it to the entire group at once.

Everyone jumped up to congratulate her with a toast to her successful career. The girls wiped their tears and vowed to have a pleasant party tonight and to put away their problems for another day.

Trystan and Isha talked about his school and her marriage. They discussed the last party five years ago.

"Do you think Dad is taping this party? Do you think he taped anything else in the last five years?" asked Isha.

"I'm not sure. Let's snoop when we know he's gone to bed tonight," suggested Trystan.

Later that night, Isha was awakened by Trystan standing over her, whispering her name. She was startled at first until she remembered their plan. Together they crept through the house into the basement. They were not surprised to see the tape recording device turned on. The women had gone to bed an hour ago, but it looked as though Mark taped them again.

Trystan searched the area thoroughly but could only come up with one condensed tape from the Christmas party and the tape from the original slumber party that Theresa had planned with the Dolphins so long ago. Mark had hidden them in the back of his locked file cabinet.

Trystan knew where Mark kept the key from previous days spying on his dad while playing detective.

"There must've been something Dad wanted to keep from the last party. There were a whole stack of tapes before, he must've played them all and taped what he wanted onto this single tape," reported Trystan.

As he was showing the tapes to Isha they heard a sound behind them. They knew they had been caught. They turned to face their father, but to their surprise, Tom and Kent were standing there. The two curious boys had followed them downstairs and were spying on the spies.

Trystan put the tapes back and locked the cabinet. He put the key back in its hiding place. They made up a story for the boys about why they were down there in the middle of the night then quickly suggested they all return to bed.

Trystan and Isha walked the boys back to their room then separated off to their own. The tapes were once again left behind.

The party ended. The Dolphins went back to their homes. Mark, Trystan and Isha flew back to New York and Ashley was left home with the twins, Lexi, and Melissa.

Chapter 4

The next five years passed quickly. There was little contact among the Dolphins. Once their kids became older, sports and other events monopolized their lives, leaving no time for anything else.

Ashley spent most of those years writing. She was turning out two books per year. Melissa was still with her, and had become very close to Arianna and Nathan. They were so different now the term twins had been put to rest.

Mark still spent most of his time in New York. Trystan married and returned to Denver. He obtained his pilot's license and purchased a small plane of his own, a Saratoga. That was not a surprise to anyone, since his passion for flying was developed at a very young age when he and Mark flew remote control planes together.

The flying hobby came to an abrupt halt in their household the day Theresa had her fatal accident. Theresa lost control of the remote control plane she was flying as it flew towards her. Before she had the opportunity to look up, the plane crashed into her skull, killing her immediately. Her family witnessed the tragic event.

Trystan stopped flying remote control planes, but his passion for flying never faded.

Isha continued to live with her husband in New York spending a great deal of time with Mark.

Both Isha and Trystan felt very uncomfortable going home to visit Ashley. Melissa made sure they did not feel welcome. Ashley thought they were imagining it, but they were sure Melissa was trying her best to drive them away.

Lexi turned twenty-five, finished school and returned to Denver to live. She married a corporate attorney with a position at a firm there.

When Isha and her husband came to visit they stayed with either Trystan or Lexi to avoid confrontation with Melissa.

The next five-year reunion Christmas party did not include Mark's kids. They agreed they were not welcome and would not be missed.

The guest list consisted of Ashley, Amy, and Stephanie. Susan did not plan to make an appearance. Dawn did not want to attend the party. Susan did not want to leave her behind. Feeling she was not the best mother for Megan she wanted to try harder to please Dawn. Megan disappeared after her release from rehab, never to speak to Susan again.

The day of the party arrived. Ashley tried to make it as festive as the two previous parties. Once again she hired a caterer and a crew to decorate the house inside and out. She made sure Nathan and Arianna rented many movies for the weekend. Now that all of the kids were nearly thirteen, the Santa appearance was over.

Much to Ashley's surprise, Mark arrived home before the guests. She was sure he would not attend. He had only been home for a few days during the entire last year. Most of that time he spent with Trystan and Lexi. At this point, Ashley did not know why they were still married. They were living separate lives. They didn't even share the same bedroom any longer when Mark did come home.

"Mark, I didn't expect you," remarked Ashley. "Are you here for the party?"

"The party? What party?" questioned Mark. "That's right, this is the weekend of your Christmas party. I'm sorry, I forgot. I'll try to stay out of your way. Are they all going to make it this year?" asked Mark, trying to get Ashley off of the subject of him coming home.

"Susan can't make it this year, but the rest will be here. What are you doing here?" asked Ashley.

"I scheduled a meeting on Monday, so I thought I would come home early and see the kids. How are Nathan and Arianna getting along?"

"They're fine. Why the sudden interest? You've ignored them for the last few years," answered Ashley.

Mark moved closer to Ashley to put his arms around her. She pushed him away.

"Ah Ash, don't be that way," pleaded Mark. "You know I've been busier these last two years than ever before in my life. I'm hoping things will slow down soon and we can spend more time together. Let's not fight every time we see each other."

Melissa, who had been listening from the next room, stepped in to break up the conversation before Ashley gave in to Mark's lies.

Melissa kept the pressure on for a divorce. She successfully forced Mark's kids out of Ashley's life. She needed a plan to get Mark to leave once and for all.

Ashley was not interested in meeting another man. Her life had become immersed in her writing, Arianna, and Nathan. She thought maybe once the kids were out on their own she might consider divorcing Mark and dating again.

"Yes Melissa, can I help you?" asked Ashley.

"I just wanted to tell you Stephanie and her boys have arrived," responded Melissa.

Ashley darted out of the room to greet Stephanie and her now very tall boys of twelve and thirteen, Tom and Kent.

Melissa shot a look of hate at Mark as he was leaving the room to pretend he was still the perfect husband and greet Stephanie. Melissa wondered, "Why the charade? Why does Mark even care what the others think? Why is he really here?"

Ashley entered the room glowing and anxious to see Stephanie. They hugged. Stephanie reintroduced the boys to Ashley. Tom was pleasant and well mannered, but Kent seemed more distant. She wondered if maybe Tom had become Stephanie's favorite and Kent was jealous. Sometimes that happens to the first born when a second child comes along.

Mark hugged Stephanie and fake punched the boys in the stomach while he commented on how they've grown.

Melissa entered the room to take everyone's coats. She was really not needed for nanny duties any longer, but stayed on to help around the house and keep Ashley from becoming lonely.

Ashley turned to Melissa and said, "Would you mind finding Arianna and Nathan to tell them Tom and Kent are here?"

Melissa left the room and returned with Arianna and Nathan.

The four teenagers left together to find something entertaining to do while Ashley and Stephanie visited.

"Is Amy here yet?" asked Stephanie nervously.

"No. Why are you so fidgety? Is something wrong?" quizzed Ashley with concern.

"No, nothing is wrong. I just have some news to share with the two of you and I hoped she would be here when I arrived," responded Stephanie. "Actually, I'm sorry Susan won't be here as well."

"What news? Tell me," begged Ashley.

"Well, oh I can't. I want to wait for Amy to get here," whined Stephanie.

At that moment they were interrupted once again by Melissa.

"We're out of nutmeg for your eggnog. Would you like me to run to the store to pick some up?" asked Melissa.

Ashley was slightly disappointed about the interruption and said, "Sure, that would be great. Why don't you check with the kids and Mark to see if they need anything before you leave."

Melissa found the group of teenagers gathered in Trystan's old room playing music and talking. After jotting down their requests for junk food she wandered off in search of Mark. Not that she wanted to do anything for him but Ashley had asked her to and she felt she should accommodate her wish.

She searched the upper level first. Mark was not in any of the bedrooms. She checked the kitchen and all the rooms on the main level. Once again he could not be found. She knew then he must have been in the basement where he hides out most of the time while he is home.

Melissa wondered what he actually did down there. So she decided to take the back stairs down to the laundry room and cut through the basement to his workshop, avoiding the stairs that lead directly to that area.

She was successful in sneaking around all of the dark corners of the basement and not bumping into anything. It was still afternoon and the sunlight cast just enough light in most of the rooms that she could find her way around without turning on lights.

Ahead, she saw the door to Mark's workshop. The door was not closed completely. She quietly walked to the door and listened for a moment before entering. She was able to peer into the room through the small gap in the door and saw Mark at this desk with his back to her.

When she heard voices she quickly jumped back, her heart racing. She was wondering how she would explain herself. She gathered her wits about her and listened more carefully. She could hear Ashley and Stephanie's voices. At first she thought they had come down the other set of stairs to visit with Mark. Then she realized Ashley was terrified of the basement and would never come down. She took a step forward for a second look into the room.

She gasped when she realized Mark was listening to the conversation Ashley and Stephanie were having. She studied him a bit longer and observed him running the tape recorder. Now she was furious. She knew he was spying on Ashley and recording it as well.

She headed back to the stairs that she came down as quickly as she could. She bumped into a box along the way and spilled its contents on the floor. She was afraid to stop to clean it up for fear Mark heard her.

She finally reached the stairs and raced to the top. Breathless at the top, she wondered why he would be doing this? Why should he care what Ashley and her friends are talking about?

She straightened her hair and took a deep breath and headed through the house to the other set of basement stairs. She slowly and with a heavy foot went down the stairs. She wanted to give Mark warning so she would not accidentally discover him. She did not want him to know that she knew what he was up to. This might be key to ending the relationship between Mark and Ashley.

Mark heard the footsteps and went to the base of the stairs as if he was about to head up. He acted startled to find Melissa there.

"I have to run an errand at the grocery store, is there anything you need?" asked Melissa nervously.

"No thanks. I'm fine," replied Mark trying to be civil to Melissa.

He wondered why she seemed so nervous. He stood on the stairs for a moment after she left to listen carefully for any sound of voices from his recording machine. He could hear nothing. He wondered if she heard anything she wasn't supposed to. He'd have to keep an eye on her. She might not buy the same story he gave

Trystan years ago about monitoring the twins when he discovered Mark had bugged the house.

Mark went back to his desk to listen to the conversation. He heard Amy come in. He started to go upstairs when he was suddenly halted by the sound of enthusiasm in Ashley's voice. He sat back down to listen.

"Amy! Oh God, I'm glad you're here. I was about to call you on your cell phone to tell you to hurry over. Stephanie has something to tell us and she wouldn't say anything, not even a hint, until you got here," exclaimed Ashley breathlessly.

Amy took off her coat and laid it across the chair. She went to the bar and poured herself a drink. The whole time she studied Stephanie's face for a clue.

She sat down and said, "Well, I'm here, let's have this earth shattering news before Ashley explodes with curiosity."

Stephanie stood up and walked over to the two of them and put her left hand out for them to look at.

"What? You found a new manicurist? Great news! I think I need another drink that news is so hard to handle," teased Amy.

Ashley screamed a blood-curdling scream. Amy was so startled she dropped her glass and it shattered all over the hardwood floor.

"What, what did I miss?" questioned Amy now more interested.

"Stephanie is engaged," screamed Ashley jumping up and down. She hugged Stephanie.

Stephanie corrected her, "No, I'm not engaged, I'm married."

"Who? When? Where?" begged Ashley.

Amy rolled her eyes in disgust as she returned to the broken glass to clean it up.

"His name is Alex, last week and we eloped," announced Stephanie. "Do you remember the last party I told you I met someone perfect but he didn't like kids? We parted ways for a few years and then re-united. We were both miserable without each other, so we ran off and got married."

"How are you going to deal with him and the boys?" asked Amy.

"The boys have matured a lot in the last five years. Alex found a wonderful boarding school for them. I think this is for the best. I've been so lonely since Richard died. I really need Alex," explained Stephanie trying to convince herself as much as them that she was doing the right thing.

Ashley asked, "How do the boys feel about this arrangement?"

"Tom is just fine with it, the boarding school idea appeals to him. He lives for school and all the events anyway, so he thinks living at school will be wonderful."

"Kent, on the other hand, is not the least bit thrilled. He doesn't like Alex and he doesn't want to go to boarding school. I guess it will just take him some time to adjust. I think that's why he is so withdrawn. I told them on the flight here today. We didn't tell them we were getting married. I thought telling them about school on the way here would help soften the blow in case they were not happy with the idea. I didn't want them to blow up or blame Alex. I'm not sure if he could handle the criticism from them. This will give them the weekend to cool off," explained Stephanie.

"I wish I could be happy for you Stephanie, I really do," sighed Amy. "But you know how I feel about men. Sounds like this Alex guy is more into himself than you and the boys. I hope it works out better for you the second time around than for Ashley and Mark."

Ashley shot a sour glance at Amy. She was always telling her what a loser Mark had turned into with her endless preaching about how worthless men are, even Mark who started out the perfect husband.

Sometimes her lecturing pressed on Ashley's nerves. Amy never missed an opportunity to condemn men. Ashley wondered what she was like in the courtroom. Was she more sympathetic to women in her courtroom than to men?

"Oh Amy, not all men are bad. Congratulations Stephanie, just ignore the man hater there. I am very happy for you and I agree the boys will eventually come around. Why didn't you bring Alex with you so we could meet him?" inquired Ashley.

"He's in Europe. He spends every Christmas season in France," reported Stephanie. "That's where his family is. I invited him to come along but he said he didn't want to break his tradition. So I guess this is probably the last Christmas party here for me. I plan to spend all my future years in Europe with Alex during the holiday season. I just had to come one last time to see you and tell you about the great new man in my life."

A few moments later Mark appeared in the room acting surprised that Amy had arrived. The friendship between Amy and Mark had cooled during the last five years. She felt Mark was no longer good for her sister Ashley.

Mark excused himself from the group. He told Ashley he made plans with Lexi.

"How is Lexi doing these days?" asked Stephanie.

"You should see her," responded Amy, "she looks exactly like Theresa. She's a good kid, but her looks make my skin crawl. I don't like to be around her."

"I know what you mean," admitted Ashley, "every time I look at her I think of Theresa. I was relieved when she moved out to go to school. Now that she's married I really don't see much of her. I feel terrible about it. We were so close when she was younger. I practically finished raising her when Mark started spending so much time in New York. It was more difficult when she began to grow up. Melissa kept coming to me with stories of Lexi being mean to the twins. I asked them about it and they always denied it but I had to wonder if any of Theresa's traits were ingrained in her personality."

Arianna, Nathan, Tom and Kent were still busy in Trystan's room listening to all his old tapes. Tom told the others that Kent has a passion for old music.

"Mark has tons of old music downstairs in the basement," reported Nathan. "He lets me listen to it all the time. Of course he won't ever let me go through it unless he's there. Wanna go see if he's down there and we can borrow some?"

Kent finally showed a spark of interest in something. He was still pretty distant after the news he received on the flight to Denver.

Nathan found his mother and asked her where Mark was because they wanted to borrow some of his music.

"He left to spend time with Lexi. You know how he feels about his privacy, so stay clear of his music until he returns," reminded Ashley.

Nathan returned to the group with the bad news. They decided to watch a movie instead.

"I'm pretty tired, I think I'll pass on the movie. I'm going back to my room to lie down for a while. I'll catch up to you guys later," yawned Kent.

He left the room and waited outside the door until he heard the movie begin. He sneaked through the house and found his way to the basement. He remembered the night he and Tom were playing spies and followed Isha and Trystan without them knowing it. He thought he could go to Mark's music collection and look through it while the others thought he was asleep.

He had a great memory for details and quickly found his way through the house to the basement. Once there he listened carefully for the sound of anyone else ahead of him before he stepped off of the last step.

He went to Mark's desk and there on the bookcase next to it he saw the recorder going. He turned up the volume a little and realized Mark was taping the women upstairs. This totally intrigued Kent. There was something about his personality. He really enjoyed the spy game and crime scenes. He watched all the television shows he could that had to do with forensics and other forms of detective work. His goal in life was to become a detective.

The recording was his first attempt at a real mystery. He searched all the drawers of Mark's desk, making sure to put every item back exactly as he found it. He had no idea what he was looking for but his adrenaline was surging at the thought of solving a crime. After all, recording someone without her knowledge is illegal, so he felt justified.

After he finished searching the desk he glanced around the room for his next task. His eyes stopped at the file cabinet standing across the room. He went to it and tried to open the top drawer. It was locked. The next three drawers were not. He searched through them and found nothing but paperwork, sheet music, and files on Mark's students.

Kent tried the top drawer again to be sure it was locked and not just jammed. It was definitely locked. The answer must be in there, thought the thirteen-year-old sleuth. He rushed back to the stairs to listen for footsteps. He heard none.

"A key, I need to find a key," he whispered.

He suddenly had a flashback to the last time he was in this room. He watched Trystan put a key back inside a trophy on a shelf. He turned quickly to see if the trophy was still there and it was. He ran over to it, took it down from the shelf and shook it upside down over his hand. Out popped the hidden key.

He rushed over to the file cabinet. He tried the key in the lock. It worked. He opened the drawer and was disappointed to see three tapes and nothing else. He picked up the tapes and read the handwritten labels that read Slumber Party, Christmas 2004, and Christmas 2009.

"What's so special about these tapes?" whispered Kent disappointedly. He was beginning to feel his crime scene had nothing to offer. Maybe Ashley had asked Mark to make these tapes so she could relive her parties.

The door at the top of the stairs opened. Kent froze for a moment. He tossed the key into the trophy, closed the file drawer but forgot to lock it. He was running out of the room when he saw the tapes sitting on the desk. He grabbed them and stuffed them in his shirt. His heart was pumping with excitement as he raced to the other staircase and ran up the stairs two by two. He walked slowly through the house so no one would bump into him running and looking guilty. He headed back upstairs to the room where he was staying. It was Isha's old room. He dropped backwards onto the bed. He felt proud of himself. He had sneaked into the crime scene, found evidence, and sneaked back out without being caught.

"This is better than television," he said in a low voice.

He laid on the bed for some time reliving his every move in his mind. Then he thought, okay, now that I have the tapes what do I do with them? He searched the room for a place to hide them in case the others came in. He noticed Isha had a stereo system that could dub copies of tapes. He dug through her desk to find blank tapes and found many packs of them. I suppose with her dad being in the recording industry, blank tapes were easy to come by in this house, he thought.

He quickly ran to the door and locked it. One by one he placed the recorded tapes in one side and a blank in the other. Soon he had made copies of all of the tapes. He felt successful. That night, when everyone was asleep, he would sneak back down and return the tapes. No one would ever know he took them. When he was safely at his new boarding school, he would have something interesting to do. He could listen to the tapes and solve the crime

74

then. For the first time since the news of the boarding school, he was anxious to go.

He joined the rest of the kids for the remainder of the day and night. They played video games and watched movies while they ate junk food. The guys started out teasing Arianna about being a girl, but she beat them easily at all the video games, gaining their respect.

Mark's footsteps were the ones Kent heard coming down the stairs. The moment Mark entered the room he noticed the light was on. He never left the light on. He went to the recorder and it was nearly finished with the tape it was recording. He changed the tape. He opened his desk drawer to drop the tape in. He looked up and saw his trophy was crooked on the shelf. He reached up to straighten it. The key was still safely hidden inside. He walked to the file cabinet and tested the lock on the top drawer. The drawer was not locked. He opened it in a panic. The tapes were gone. Immediately he remembered Melissa and how nervous she was acting. She must be responsible, thought Mark.

He paced the floor wondering what he was going to do. He had to stop her before she gave those tapes to Ashley. Mark shut off the light and went outdoors to pace and think before he joined Ashley and her friends. He didn't want to give her the opportunity to be alone with Melissa.

He watched Melissa's every move for the rest of the evening.

That night, when everyone in the house was asleep, Kent crept through the house, making his way down the stairs to return the tapes and lock the file cabinet.

After Kent left the room, Mark went back down and looked around the room to see if the tapes were still in the room. He walked back to the file cabinet to open the top drawer again. He was hoping since the tapes were dark colored and the file cabinet was black that he just panicked when it was unlocked and the tapes had slid to the back of the drawer and were still there. This time, the drawer was locked. He retrieved the key, unlocked the drawer and found the tapes.

If Melissa had the tapes earlier in the day, Mark's presence at the party foiled her plan to give them to Ashley.

"She probably plans to give them to her in the morning," he thought.

Ashley woke the next morning to find Stephanie making coffee in the kitchen.

"Want some?" asked Stephanie when Ashley walked in.

"Sure, but why are you making the coffee? Where's Melissa?" yawned Ashley.

"I'm not sure. I haven't seen her. The kitchen was empty when I came down, so I thought I would start the coffee," explained Stephanie.

Ashley looked at the clock. It was eight o'clock. Melissa always arrived by seven-thirty.

Mark entered the kitchen.

"Where's Melissa? Shouldn't she be making breakfast by now?" quizzed Mark.

"That's what I was wondering," said Ashley.

Mark fixed breakfast for everyone. The crowd devoured everything Mark prepared. As he was cleaning the kitchen the phone rang.

Ashley answered, "Hello. Yes, this is Ashley. Oh Jordan, we were just wondering where your mom was. Is she ill today?"

Ashley listened to what Jordan had to say and turned white.

"No! Oh God no!" she screamed.

Mark took the phone, "Jordan this is Mark Wilson. Is there a problem?"

Jordan repeated the story to Mark.

He said, "If you need anything please don't hesitate to call. We'd like to help in any way we can."

He hung up the phone.

Stephanie walked back into the room to find Ashley sobbing on the floor. She looked at Mark for an explanation.

"Melissa's brakes failed. She was killed in an accident on her way home last night," reported Mark.

Chapter 5

Luckily, Mark and Stephanie were with Ashley, trying to comfort her in any way they could. When Michael died, or was murdered, Ashley had her friends around her to ease the pain. Melissa meant so much to Ashley. She was really going to miss her.

Mark kept checking his watch. Even through her veil of tears Ashley was aware he wanted to leave.

"If you have somewhere you need to be, just go," she blurted out with anger in her voice. "Stephanie will be here for me."

Mark tried to explain, "No, I'll stay with you but I should call Lexi and tell her what happened and that I won't be over to see her today."

"Go, just go. I want you to go. I don't want to see you right now. You can't feel my pain. You didn't even like Melissa. You've been wanting to fire her for a long time now," screamed Ashley, striking out at Mark.

Mark glanced at Stephanie and shrugged his shoulders.

"I'll stay here with her. Just run along. I don't think you being here when she is so angry and hurt is helping the matter," agreed Stephanie in a sympathetic tone.

Mark reached down for Ashley's hand, "Would you like me to tell the twins?"

Ashley didn't even answer. She just glared at Mark. He knew it would be best to leave immediately. He was preparing to do so when the doorbell rang.

Arianna called out, "I'll get it," as she ran to the door.

Mark drew back the lace curtains as he glanced out the second story window. A police car was parked along the curb in front of the house. He was anxious to leave without getting delayed answering questions about Melissa. He planned to slip out the back door. He knew the police would come in the front door. His plan was to casually get into his car to drive away unnoticed.

Arianna stood there for a moment, looking out the door beyond the two men at the car parked in the driveway. She looked up at the two men and asked, "Can I help you? Do you want to talk to my mom or dad?"

Nathan walked into the room with the two other young people.

"Mark just left. I watched him grab his music bag and leave out the back door. I'll run to catch him."

The two officers stepped inside the door.

A tall sandy blond detective with green eyes tired from lack of sleep started the conversation, "My name is Detective Karst and this is Officer Thompson."

Arianna shook hands with both men.

Detective Karst went on, "Is your mother or father available to speak with us about Melissa Rivas? We have a few questions for them."

Nathan returned. Arianna was confused. Tom was nervous but Kent was excited.

"Wow, what'd she do? Are you gonna arrest her?" asked Kent bursting with enthusiasm.

"I'm afraid there's been an accident," replied Officer Thompson.

He was much younger than Detective Karst and was far from the seasoned expert that Detective Karst had become. He had dark hair that was cut too short to be attractive; it gave him a stiff hard appearance. He never smiled while on duty. Thompson looked the picture of physical fitness, but if the truth were known, the years of working out and practicing Russian martial arts made the older Detective Karst the more powerful and cunning of the two.

Tom searched the main level of the house for his mother and Ashley. He ran upstairs and found the two of them in Ashley's room. He wanted to be the first to tell them about Melissa's accident but he could tell by all the tears that the news had already reached Ashley.

"There are two policemen downstairs that want to talk to Mrs. Wilson," Tom reported.

Stephanie and Ashley followed Tom along the hall and down the wide curved wooden staircase. As Ashley made her entrance with Stephanie, Detective Karst looked up at her. He immediately remembered that not only had he been in this house before but also Ashley was the same woman he had interviewed, once for the death of Brian, Susan's husband, and once for the death of her own husband, Michael. That was many years ago.

Ashley did not recognize Detective Karst. Karst had a keen ability to remember facts from all of his cases. It was as if he stored every bit of data in a central computer system in his brain for future reference. That would probably explain why he has trouble letting a case grow cold and unsolved. The data keeps re-circulating, not allowing him to delete it or put it to rest.

"I'm sure you are here to ask questions about Melissa," remarked Ashley.

Karst responded, "Yes ma'am, I can see you are under much stress at the moment so we'll be as brief as possible and try to get out of your hair quickly."

Ashley and Stephanie continued into the room and sat on the sofa. Karst and Thompson resumed their seats and began with the questioning.

"We spoke with Jordan, Mrs. Rivas' daughter, this morning. She said Mrs. Rivas was coming home from your house last evening when she had her accident. She

81

said she's worked for you for many years. She said she was your nanny. Is all of this correct so far?" inquired Detective Karst.

Ashley seemed to be staring past him while he spoke and did not indicate in any way that she agreed or disagreed with his comments.

"Yes, you are correct. I hired her about twelve years ago as my nanny. The twins are older now and don't really need a nanny, but I kept Melissa on as a personal companion. She ran errands for me and did light housekeeping or just helped out wherever necessary. She was more of a friend to me than an employee," replied Ashley choking on her last sentence.

Stephanie handed her another tissue and put her arm around her.

"What exactly happened? Does any one know yet?" asked Stephanie.

"It's too early to tell much about foul play at this point. We will know more in a day or two," stated Thompson in a very professional tone.

Detective Karst furrowed his brow. Sometimes he preferred to go on his interviews alone so he could be less stiff and more sympathetic to the people that he interviewed. He found if he took a gentle approach he lessened the chance of causing unnecessary pain and could actually retrieve more information if the person he is interviewing remains calm.

82

Kent leaped up to get closer to Detective Karst.

"Foul play? Did someone kill Melissa?" insisted Kent.

Detective Karst turned to Kent and said, "We're assuming Melissa's brakes failed accidentally until we know otherwise."

"You'll have to excuse Kent, Detective Karst, he's totally fascinated with crime scenes and police work. It's become his passion," explained Stephanie. "I'm curious though, surely no one intended to indicate that this was anything more than an accident, right?"

How quickly the past came to the present. Fifteen years ago the Dolphins were in this very house discussing murder versus accident. Fifteen years ago in this house the murders of six innocent husbands were schemed and plotted. One glance at Ashley revealed the same thoughts going through her mind. It was a good thing Detective Karst could not read their minds or much more than a car accident investigation would be going on.

"Well ma'am, we just like to cover all angles, that's just part of our job," said Detective Karst evasively.

He turned back to Ashley.

"Did Mrs. Rivas generally leave your home in the evenings and return to work in the morning by seven-thirty? That seems to be more than your typical eight hour shift."

"We were having a Christmas party and Melissa was both helping out and a guest. She just hung around for the entertainment. She was free to leave whenever she wanted," explained Ashley, wondering if he thought she took advantage of her because she was a minority working for a rich white woman.

Stephanie jumped to attention, "You do suspect something, what's going on?"

Once again Detective Karst had hoped for a more subtle line of questioning.

"Actually, there was no brake fluid in her car. We realize a brake line could've broken or something could've been old and worn or damaged. There are a number of things that could have caused the fluid to drain. Maybe she had warnings but ignored them and should've had her brakes checked or more fluid put in," suggested Detective Karst to take the seriousness out of the discussion.

"Whoa! Someone cut her brake lines. Melissa was murdered. Who could've had the motive and opportunity?" piped in Kent looking into the eyes of everyone in the room as he accused them of taking part.

Arianna could no longer control her emotions. Melissa was like a second mother to her. Nathan was trying to be manly but he too was about to break.

Ashley noticed this and sent Nathan to take Arianna to her room and stay with her.

Stephanie took Kent aside to lecture him. Tom remained silent in a chair watching the whole scene. He was very nervous. This event was disturbing to him.

"You do realize this is all routine ladies, and I have to ask these questions. Can I have a list of your guests from last night?" requested Detective Karst, trying to get back on track with his questions.

"There's not really a list," started Ashley. "The kids were here, Stephanie, Melissa and myself. My sister Amy was here. I guess you would know her as Judge Amy Roth and ..."

"Judge Roth is your sister?" asked Thompson. "She's one tough judge. I'd hate to be a man accused of something in her courtroom. She's pretty merciless at times."

Ashley just looked at him blinking her eyes. She was a little surprised by his comment, not that she did not agree, but because he actually said it to her.

"That's all for now. If you have any questions or can think of anything we should know, here's my card. I'm pretty sure we won't be back to bother you. Once again, please accept my apologies for having to intrude at such a delicate time." With that, Detective Karst headed for the door.

He paused, turned around and returned to the room. He walked over to Kent, who was feeling badly about being scolded. He put his hand out to shake his and patted him on the shoulder with the opposite hand.

"Hang in there Kent, I think you have a great future on the force. If there is ever anything I can do to help you along when you're older, please look me up. I've been here for so many years I don't plan on leaving," said Detective Karst kindly.

"Unless you get killed or something," Kent pointed out to him.

Stephanie dropped to the sofa with her face in her hands. Half of her wanted to die of embarrassment the other half wanted to laugh.

Detective Karst did laugh as he strolled back to the door.

"We're gonna take a quick look around outside before we go. Can anyone tell me where Mrs. Rivas was parked last night?" questioned Detective Karst.

"Under the carport on the side of the house," said Ashley.

Once outside Detective Karst and Officer Thompson checked the concrete where the car had been parked. The driveway was wide enough for two and a half cars. It went through the carport and curved around behind the house to a three-car garage.

"Whew!" whistled Thompson, "This is some place. I wonder what her old man does for a living?"

Detective Karst did not answer.

Thompson repeated himself, "Nice place huh? Where do they get their bucks?"

"Oh, she's a pretty famous mystery novelist. I'm not sure if she remarried," responded Detective Karst with his mind elsewhere.

"How'd you know she's a writer?" asked Thompson. "She never mentioned it?"

"I've been here before on two separate occasions to investigate deaths. I remembered her," Karst explained.

He still had his mind off somewhere; the somewhere was years ago.

"It was about fifteen years ago when I was still a rookie detective. I got called into this case downtown at the Adam's Mark Hotel. Seems this rich guy had a little too much to drink. He had this really nasty allergy to latex. He was at this Trekkie convention..."

"A what convention?" asked Thompson.

"A Star Trek convention," replied Detective Karst. "Anyway, he accidentally picked up the wrong mask and put it on. He wore it back to his room and passed out on the bed from the booze. He never woke up. He died of anaphylactic shock. His throat just swelled shut and his face was all red and blotchy and swollen."

Detective Karst stood there for a moment gazing back at the house rubbing his hand under his chin.

"That was one odd case. I mean, I just couldn't quite figure out how it happened. Think about it. How many drunks are hauled in who still manage to find their own car in a crowded lot, find the keys, start the ignition, and make it home? Why would this guy have been any different? Your average drunk doesn't even think he is putting himself or any one else in danger. If you can be slightly coherent enough while drunk to master those small tasks, why couldn't you double check your mask before putting it on when it could mean life or death?"

He looked back at the house one last time as he walked to the car. Their search of the grounds had revealed nothing.

"What was the second time for?" asked Thompson interested in the lives of the rich and famous.

Detective Karst came back from his world of thought to answer, "Let's see, it was a few months later. Mrs. Moore's husband died of an asthma attack at the gym playing ball with some college kids. Not much to tell there, just an accident."

"Well it says here in my notes that your Mrs. Moore is really Mrs. Wilson. Hey old man, you're finally slipping. A name escaped your memory. Will wonders never cease," he teased.

"What? Are you sure? I know I'm right. She must've remarried. I wonder where her husband is?" questioned Detective Karst.

"Maybe that's who the boy was going after when we got there. He called him Mark and the girl called him dad. So who owns the kids? I specifically remember Mrs. Wilson calling them twins," bragged Thompson feeling pretty good about himself. It is not often he can present information into a case that Karst has not already beaten him to.

Once back at the office Detective Karst sent Thompson off to check the progress of the car for an answer about the brake line.

As soon as he was out of sight Detective Karst unlocked the bottom drawer to his desk. Since he made detective and especially during his rookie days he kept the files of cases that didn't feel right to him in the locked drawer.

He would take them home with him on occasion and go over them trying to find something he could've missed. He found the file marked Brian Saunders. He flipped it open; it read "cause of death accidental". He thumbed through it for a minute to see if there was something that jumped out at him.

Thompson showed up at Detective Karst's desk. Detective Karst quickly replaced the file. He was on the clock now; this was not his personal time.

"What's up?" he asked Thompson.

"Nothing's conclusive. They can't say it definitely was an accident. I'm not a mechanic, but they said something about a loose screw and the road dirt not matching, for whatever that's worth," reported Thompson with a coffee in one hand and a stack of Christmas cookies in the other.

"You're the one with a screw loose. I guess I'd better go talk to the guys myself," said Detective Karst, annoyed.

Detective Karst grabbed his jacket and headed toward the door. He walked through the garage to find the person in charge of the Rivas car. The guys in the shop were whistling and teasing him. They were bowing down.

Usually, the big shot detectives would just call from their desks and demand a report, but to have a special visit from Karst was an honor, they joked. He liked to follow through on even the smallest detail when he had the opportunity. This is one of those rare times when his workload was a little lighter than normal.

Bill, the man Karst needed to talk to, met him at the car.

"What do you have for me?" asked Detective Karst.

"I wish what I have could be more conclusive one way or the other, Glen," responded Bill. "Look here, see this screw right here? It's loose, very loose. All of the fluid drained out. There was no hope of stopping this car. By the way the road rash looked there was no sign of braking only yaw marks. This car had no brakes when this lady needed them."

"Yeah, that's what the eyewitnesses said. They said she ran the red light and swerved all over the road. At first they thought she had passed out or was drunk. She tried really hard to keep the car on the road but lost it at the concrete overpass. Anyway, what do you mean you can't give me an answer? What are my choices?" questioned Karst.

"Typically a screw like this does not jiggle itself loose. The fact that she just had the car serviced could answer your question. It's possible this screw was not tightened properly and gradually worked its way to being even more loose. It's possible it's been loose for some time

90

and the mechanics didn't catch it. The screw on this side has less road grunge on it than the one on the other side. That can mean it was recently tampered with, or someone at the scene ran their gloved hand under here to check for a leak and cleaned some of the gunk off in the process," explained Bill.

"Think about it. Who would want to do in a fifty-five-year-old woman with no money? I think she either had some really bad luck or a really bad mechanic. Too bad," admitted Bill.

"I guess you're right. I can't come up with a motive; no sign of anything at the site the car was last parked. No enemies, just a bunch of people who will miss her a lot. I guess this one is just another auto fatality making it on this side of the New Year."

"I think I'll head home. Debby is going to love you for not finding anything. I promised her this year we would make it to Hawaii. She doesn't believe me. She knew a case would come up before tomorrow and she couldn't pull me away. She says even if we make it and we're sunning ourselves on the beach and a dead fish floats up, I'll be on the case leaving her alone in Hawaii," moaned Karst feeling she exaggerated a bit.

"She's really got you pegged," laughed Bill.

Detective Karst turned to walk away.

Bill called after him, "Hey those dead fish, toss them to the sharks. Better an unsolved fish death than Debby throwing you to the sharks!" laughed Bill.

Detective Karst raised his hand over his head to wave good-bye without looking back. "Merry Christmas," he called out.

He was going home to pack and leave in the morning and had no intentions of looking back until he returned from his vacation.

Mark returned later in the day. Ashley had been dealing with a world of emotions. Mark was the last person she wanted to see. She went up to her room and told Stephanie to tell him she did not want to be disturbed.

Stephanie passed the message on.

Stephanie's kids popped in to bring Mark up to speed on the events of the day. Arianna and Nathan were still feeling badly and did not want to come down. Tom stood next to Kent beaming at him waiting for him to tell the story in true Kent style.

Not only was Kent an avid reader of mysteries and crime magazines, but also he never missed a good show on the subject. He had the ability to embellish a story to make it sound better than life.

Stephanie said, "Kent, don't bother Mark with your details. I'm sure he has better things to do." She felt Mark might want to disappear to his basement haven to avoid being sociable to a house full of people under the present circumstances.

"No, really, it's fine. Tell away, my boy, and spare no details," teased Mark.

92

Kent had the stage. He acted out everyone's parts. He told the story in such painstaking detail that even his brother Tom, who idolized him, left to go find something better to do.

Stephanie went upstairs to pack; Kent had Mark all to himself. After Kent gave his complete run down, Mark asked him to repeat more about the questions the police asked and if they found anything outside.

Kent was so excited that Mark was so interested that he went into the entire story all over again.

Stephanie and Tom came down carrying luggage.

"It's time to go," reported Stephanie. "Run up and pack your things and meet us at the car."

Kent moaned as he climbed the stairs. This was the best family vacation he could remember. He found secret recordings, and a possible murder all in one weekend. At least there was a dead body, he thought.

Once back in the guest room he packed his things and removed the duplicate tapes from among the others in the drawer with the blank tapes. He thought hiding the tapes along with a drawer full of other tapes was brilliant. Sometimes he wondered if he would be better off being the criminal or the detective. He knew his keen criminal mind would make him good on either side of the law.

Soon all the bags were packed into the car. Ashley stayed in her room to avoid Mark. Stephanie ran up to say good-bye. Nathan, Arianna and Mark said their good-byes in the driveway.

The departure was exceptionally hard for Stephanie. She knew she could come back for a visit any time she wanted, but this was the last Christmas party now that she was married to Alex. Parties she attended in that house spanned forty years.

The years had been good to her and her friends. They were aging nicely, some would say. They were in their forties, so if one of them died in the next ten years or so, at least then the thought of murder wouldn't have to creep into their thoughts before each funeral.

They loaded into the car and waved as they left the driveway.

Once inside the house Mark ran downstairs to check his tapes. He knew that if Kent had left off any details the entire conversation would be on the tape he put in before he left.

Since Ashley wasn't speaking to Mark, he decided to pack his things and spend the night with Lexi and her husband. After his meeting the next day, he would return to New York.

Ashley stood at her window watching Mark load the car and drive away. She was angry that he left her alone, but she didn't want his company. She watched his car shrink from her sight as he drove further down the street away from her. This time she really felt he had gone away. Until now she had Melissa and her work to keep her going. She could not forget Arianna and Nathan, but soon they will be on their own as well.

She whispered, "What am I waiting for? Mark's not a father to the twins. He's not a husband to me and I'm no longer a wife for him. I have all of the money I need."

She walked to the mirror to look at herself. The once sparkling white blond hair was not so sparkling. Around her eyes were the tiniest signs of wrinkles to come.

"Ashley old girl, you're not getting any younger. Take your life back. It's time for the big D".

That night at dinner Ashley broke the news to her kids. She was not sure what to expect. She had not allowed herself the opportunity to ever think about herself until they were well established on their own. To her surprise, they were very understanding.

"We were wondering how much longer you would wait," admitted Arianna.

"Yeah, Melissa has been telling us for years that you and Mark were not happy and that you would be better off without him," reported Nathan.

Unfortunately, once Mark moved back to New York, the plan for divorce did not take priority in Ashley's life.

Amy spent as much time with her as she could, which was not much. The kids were getting busier with school. Ashley was trying to write more than the two books in a year. But she was still lonely.

She had become so accustomed to Melissa handling her calls and all the little tasks she did around the house for her that things were falling apart, bit-by-bit.

Ashley did have a housekeeper that came in, but she did not have the personal duties that Melissa had.

Amy helped her search for a new personal assistant. She found a nice young lady in her thirties who needed day work while her kids were in school. She studied journalism and had read all of Ashley's books, so it was a good match. Ashley hired Carol.

Amy took Carol aside and said, "The first order of business after you have her meetings and calls in order is to help her divorce Mark once and for all. Take her by the hand and make her pack up his things and send them to him. I'll make an appointment with an attorney friend of mine and we'll get my sister's life in order."

That's exactly what happened. Room by room, Mark's belongings were removed and packed into boxes to be shipped along with the divorce papers. That was Amy's idea; a stronger statement would be made that way.

The entire house was finished except for the basement. Amy and Ashley sat on the sofa looking at each other.

Amy offered, "If you can't do it, I'd be happy to. No one says you have to face the ghost of your dad in the basement."

"I say I have to," insisted Ashley. "I'm going to do it. So go home and let me do it alone."

Carol had empty boxes in each room. Ashley took the laundry room stairs to the basement to avoid the stairs her dad was on when he fell to his death. Item by item she filled boxes. When she came to the file cabinet she couldn't find the key to the top drawer so she emptied the remaining drawers. As she emptied the bookshelves she found the key, it rattled in the trophy as she tipped it to place it into a box.

Happy that she found the key she opened the drawer. She removed the tapes and slowly read the labels.

"What in the world," she whispered wondering what was on the tapes. She had already packed Mark's music equipment. She took the tapes to the kitchen and put in the first slumber party tape. It had been edited and only contained the part about plotting the murders of all the husbands.

Ashley's fingers were trembling as she fumbled for the buttons to make it stop, to make the memories go away.

Chapter 6

Every part of Ashley felt ill. Her stomach ached with sharp pains; her heart was racing out of control. Fragments of thoughts were rushing through her mind so quickly she could not grab one to focus on. She paced back and forth in the kitchen. She ran through the house up the stairs to her room. She closed the door and locked it behind her. She needed to feel safe.

She sat on her bed hugging a pillow to her chest trying to think. She rocked back and forth in an attempt to comfort herself. Finally, she took a deep breath and reached for the phone. She dialed Amy's number. Amy didn't answer. She tried her cell phone. It rang and rang until when Ashley was about to hang up she heard Amy's voice.

"Hello," said Amy.

Ashley responded with a trembling voice, "Amy, where are you? You need to get over here right away. He knows."

"Who knows what?" asked Amy.

"Just get over here, hurry!" screamed Ashley.

"I'm getting my hair cut; my hair's dripping. Can it wait an hour?" asked Amy.

"No! Come right now," yelled Ashley gasping for air.

"Okay, I'll be right there," agreed Amy as she hung up the phone and grabbed a towel for her wet hair.

Amy explained to her stylist that there was a family emergency; she had to leave. She paid her for her services thus far and told her she would return the towel.

Amy raced to her car and sped to Ashley's house hoping it would not be the day she'd get stopped for speeding.

When Amy arrived at Ashley's house, she rang the bell, but when Ashley didn't come immediately to the door she used her key to let herself in. She met Ashley on the stairs.

"What's going on?" demanded Amy.

"Shhh...," whispered Ashley with her fingers to her lips. "Let's go out to your car."

Once out in the car, Amy was becoming a little less patient. She wanted to know what was so important that she had to leave her hair appointment with wet hair and go out into the freezing weather.

"Well?" she asked.

Ashley was trembling from fear, not the cold winter air.

"I went into the basement...," she started.

Amy cut in, "I knew I should've gone down there with you. It was too much for you, wasn't it?"

"No, that's not it. I was packing Mark's things when I found these."

She handed Amy the tapes she found locked in Mark's file cabinet.

"That's it? Tapes have you this worked up?" complained Amy.

"Mark knows about the murders from the slumber party. This tape has our voices planning the murders."

"What do you mean our voices, the murders? I'm confused," responded Amy.

"You need to listen to it," cried Ashley.

"Okay, okay calm down. Let's go back inside and listen," suggested Amy.

"No, I don't want to go back inside. Mark had the house bugged," whined Ashley. "I think I disconnected everything but I'm not sure. Let's go to your house in case I'm wrong or he shows up."

"Are you expecting him to?"

"No, I don't know. I just don't want to take any chances. He had these locked up and I found the key and I don't want him to know I have them. I don't know why he never told me," Ashley was rambling.

Amy started the engine of her car and they drove to her house. She wanted to dry her hair first, but Ashley wouldn't let her.

They went into her living room and Amy poured a couple of drinks for them before she put a tape on. Together they sat on the floor with their backs against the sofa facing the tape player as it began to release their voices from the night of the slumber party.

They sat there in silence while they heard themselves drunkenly plan all the deaths. This tape was edited to make it sound as if they were actually making plans to carry through with the murders. It also refreshed their foggy memories about exactly what was said that night.

"Oh shit!" exclaimed Amy. "This is bad. This is incriminating. No one would believe we didn't commit those murders with this tape as evidence. This is really, really bad."

Amy downed her drink. She went back to her bar and poured another. She downed it just as quickly and poured a third. She began to pace the room.

Ashley kept her eyes on Amy as she paced. Neither or them spoke. Ashley gathered her knees to her chest and held them in place with her arms and began to rock again.

Ashley broke the silence, "What are we going to do?"

Amy went to Ashley and sat on the floor in front of her. She set her glass down and unwrapped Ashley's arms.

"Let's be rational here. Let's think this through. First, how did Mark tape us that night, and why?" asked Amy.

"Well, Mark wasn't even there that night. The storm kept everyone away. The power was out, so he couldn't have taped us without electricity," responded Ashley pulling it together now.

"Okay, you're right. We were alone there, the six of us. Mark wasn't there and the power was out. Let's think back to that night. How could a tape recording of our conversation have been made without our knowledge?" questioned Amy.

"I've got it!" shouted Amy as she jumped to her feet. She ran across the room to her entertainment center and rifled through her CD cases. She pulled out the CD Theresa had sent her for Christmas shortly after the slumber party. She held it up for Ashley to see.

"Oh my God, I'd forgotten about the CD. We were being taped and it was with our knowledge. We used Susan's tape recorder to tape us singing that ridiculous song while we were drunk," reminded Ashley.

"Yep, Susan's recorder was going. Theresa ended up with the tape. She must've taken it home to make copies for us," explained Amy on a roll now.

"I'll bet she had Mark make the copies with all of his recording equipment in the basement," stated Ashley.

"The tape must've still been running while we played the murder game. Mark must've known all along. But if he knew then why didn't he stop Theresa from killing everyone? Why didn't he come to us or go to the police? Why did he remain quiet like the rest of us? And why did he keep the tape?" questioned Amy, using her criminal attorney mind.

"I'm not sure I can answer any of those questions. What would he have to gain by keeping it secret?" asked Ashley. " Unless he wanted to protect Theresa the same way we all wanted to protect ourselves."

"That's a good point," agreed Amy. "But if he wanted to protect Theresa, why didn't he destroy the tape? Why did he keep it all these years under lock and key? Is he planning to use it against us in some way?"

"I think we need to tell the others. Don't you agree?" asked Ashley.

"I'm not sure what good it will do, but I guess they have a right to know. I just don't think it's such a good idea to include Brittany, since she doesn't have a clue about any of this. So what do we do? Should we just spring this to them on the phone?" asked Amy.

"Well, they're on opposite ends of the country. I don't know what else we can do," responded Ashley.

"This time of day we'd probably find both of them at their offices. Use my phone in the den and you call

Susan. I'll use my cell phone and I'll call Stephanie. Let's see if they'd be available for a conference call within the hour. Let's say three o'clock Mountain Time," suggested Amy.

Ashley agreed, "That should work."

They made their calls.

Ashley placed a call to Susan's office. Amy had her number in her address book. Susan's receptionist told her she was with a client and she would be busy the rest of the day. Ashley pushed her a little harder and told her it was an emergency that she must interrupt and that Susan would understand.

The receptionist put Ashley on hold while she went in to hand a note to Susan.

Susan picked up the phone "Ashley, what's wrong?"

"Plenty. Will you be available for a conference call with Amy, and Stephanie and me in about thirty minutes?" asked Ashley with a very anxious tone to her voice.

"I'm afraid not. I have another client then. Actually, I'm booked for the entire day. Can it wait until this evening?" pleaded Susan.

"No, we need to talk soon. Mark has a tape of all of us plotting the murders at the slumber party. We need to deal with this immediately."

"How did he get a tape of that? What are you talking about?" insisted Susan.

"Not now. Can we count on you for the conference call or not?" asked Ashley.

"Yes, of course. I'll tell my receptionist to reschedule the rest of the day. I'll be waiting by the phone. Talk to you then," sighed Susan as she hung up the phone.

Amy was able to get right through to Stephanie. Their conversation was nearly identical to the one Ashley and Susan had.

Amy poured herself another drink. She offered one to Ashley, but Ashley refused.

"Take it easy with that stuff. We need you to be able to think clearly," scolded Ashley.

"Yeah, that's easy for you to say. Can you imagine what will happen if this leaks out? Judge Roth convicted of not one but five murders? Do you know how many people I would meet in prison that I sent there?"

"Now, calm down. It's been fifteen years and Mark hasn't done anything with the tape so far why would he now?" reminded Ashley.

Amy sat on the sofa tapping her foot nervously on the floor while she watched the clock. Ashley was the one pacing now.

"Okay, it's time. Make the call. I'll go use the phone in the kitchen," insisted Ashley.

Amy dialed all the necessary numbers to make the call complete. Stephanie and Susan were on the line.

Stephanie, after greeting everyone said, "What in the hell is going on?"

"Yes," agreed Susan, "give us the whole story."

Ashley began, "I've decided to divorce Mark. Carol, my new personal assistant, and I have been going from room to room in the house packing Mark's things to send to him. I went into the basement to finish. One of the drawers of his file cabinet was locked. At first I couldn't find the key. When I did find the key and unlocked the drawer all that was in it were some tapes. They were labeled slumber party, and all the Christmas parties we had. I was curious about them, so I went upstairs and played the slumber party tape. It was edited to make it sound like we were really planning the murders and they happened just as we planned."

"Why does Mark have these tapes?" asked Susan.

"That's what we're trying to figure out," replied Amy.

"What's on the other tapes?" asked Stephanie.

Ashley and Amy shot glances across the room at each other. Ashley took the kitchen phone into the living room to join Amy.

"I don't know," replied Ashley. "After I heard the first one I never listened to the rest."

"Don't you think we should listen to them? Maybe we'd be able to understand more about what's going on," suggested Stephanie.

Amy took the tapes from Ashley's coat and played the first one. Once again the tape was edited. The only portion of the conversation recorded was discussion about the murders.

"That's too weird," said Stephanie.

Susan agreed, "Obviously Mark has some plan for these tapes. Now that Theresa is dead, it has to go beyond protecting her."

"Why don't we just burn the tapes? Then there will be no way to connect us to anything," suggested Stephanie.

"Burning the tapes could cause Mark to make a move," stated Amy. "We don't know where the master tapes are. For all we know he could have a set with him in New York. If he comes home and the tapes are missing, there's no telling what he'll do."

"How does he feel about the divorce?" asked Susan. "Will that cause him to flare up and strike out?"

"He doesn't know about the divorce. We were going to pack his things and send them with the divorce papers," admitted Ashley.

"That sounds a little severe. Don't tell me, that one was your idea, right Amy?" remarked Stephanie.

Amy responded, "Guilty as charged. I thought the jerk should have a nasty surprise in store for him the way he's neglected Ashley and the twins these last few years."

Susan jumped in, "For heaven's sake, don't do that now. We surely don't want him angry. Maybe you should unpack his things and replace the tapes until we can figure out what's going on. We've kept our secret for fifteen years; now is not the time to panic."

They all agreed that would be their immediate plan. Amy and Ashley told the others they would listen to all the tapes and make copies of them before they returned them to the file cabinet. A phone date was set for the next afternoon. Stephanie didn't want Alex to overhear her conversation and Susan wanted to protect Dawn from the information. Calling at their offices was the best plan.

Amy and Ashley, wasting no time, began to listen to the remaining tapes. They were all the same. They were edited to contain only conversations the Dolphins had in private at Ashley's house about the murders. Until they listened to the last tape. This tape contained the unedited version of the police interview with Detective Karst about Melissa's car accident.

"That's curious. Why would he be interested in what the police had to say about Melissa's accident? What has that got to do with the rest of the murders?" asked Ashley.

"I'm not sure, but there must be some connection. We need to get these tapes copied and returned to the cabinet. I don't have any blank tapes. I just use CD's. I'll run to the store to grab some," reported Amy.

"There are plenty of them at my house. The kids used to put cases of them in their rooms. Mark would buy them for his work and his kids would just help themselves," stated Ashley.

They gathered the tapes and drove back to Ashley's house.

As soon as they arrived they tore off their coats and ran to Isha's room. Ashley was right. Isha had an entire drawer full of blank tapes. Ashley was relieved Isha left her old tape player behind. They were able to dub the tapes in a very short amount of time. Once the tapes were locked in place in the file cabinet they both breathed a sigh of relief.

Amy helped Ashley unpack the things from Mark's work area downstairs. Ashley was having a hard time remembering where everything went. This was only the second time she had gone down there and was not familiar at all with the room.

When it came time to hook up all the sound equipment again they were both at a loss.

"What will we do now?" asked Ashley in a panic. "I don't know how to connect all of these wires."

"Well don't look at me. I have trouble plugging my hair blower in," exaggerated Amy.

Amy and Ashley were sitting on the floor amidst a sea of tangled wires trying to sort through them like one would untangle a string of Christmas lights when the door at the top of the stairs opened.

A gasp came from both of them. They didn't know if they should stay put or run for the other staircase.

Either way they were going to be caught so they opted to stay put.

Step by step they listened to the footsteps on the stairs as they approached the bottom. They looked up to see Carol entering the room.

"I thought you might be down here when I couldn't find you anywhere else in the house," reported Carol.

Ashley and Amy both sighed a huge sigh of relief.

"Did I frighten the two of you? I'm sorry, I should've called down the stairs first," apologized Carol. She remembered how frightened Ashley was of the basement, and felt badly for startling her.

Ashley admitted, "Well we were a little startled, but no need to apologize. Say, how are you with all of this electrical stuff? Can you figure out how to connect all of these wires?"

Carol laughed, "Oh my no, I wouldn't know where to begin. I leave all of that stuff to my son. He's a kid genius when it comes to that stuff."

"Do you suppose kid genius would mind coming over and helping us out?" asked Amy.

"I could ask him," responded Carol.

"Could you ask him now?" pleaded Amy.

Ashley spoke up, "I was a little hasty moving Mark's things out. I've decided to be a little more gentle with my approach and discuss the divorce with him and let him pack his own things. I feel badly now and would like to put everything back in its place but I don't know how."

"I understand. I'll go call him and ask him to come over," said Carol as she went upstairs to make the call.

"Boy you're such a good liar. I almost believed you," laughed Amy.

Carol made the call to her son and returned to the basement to help Amy and Ashley unpack the boxes.

It was less than thirty minutes later when Carol's son, Dillon, arrived. He went right to the task of plugging all the wires into the correct places. He began putting all the equipment back into its place.

Ashley said, "I'm not sure where everything goes so your guess is as good as mine."

"I think I can remember where most of it goes," reported Dillon.

Before Ashley could respond an embarrassed Carol admitted, "When I saw all of the equipment Mr. Wilson had down here I told Dillon about it. He begged me to let him come and look at it so one day when I knew you were out for the day I let him come over."

Ashley walked over to Carol and put her arm around her and said, "Bless you Carol, I'm so glad you did. Now maybe we can get this room back into shape."

The three women unboxed all of the items that Ashley had packed. Dillon put the sound equipment back together and moved a few of the items around on the desk and the shelves to the spots he remembered them in when he spent the afternoon studying the room and all the equipment. He had made a mental image of much of it because he hoped someday to have the same setup for himself.

It was time for Carol and Dillon to go home by the time the basement was finished. Ashley thanked them both again and slipped Dillon some money for his help. At first, he declined, but when Ashley told him it was a down payment on his future equipment, he took it with a smile and thanked her.

Amy and Ashley called for Chinese takeout. They sat down to listen to the tapes again, searching for clues. Everything on the tapes just made them look guilty. There was nothing that would give them any indication of why Mark wanted to tape them in the first place and why he edited them to reveal only the murders.

They listened to the tapes again. The doorbell rang; they both jumped. Ashley went to the door and Amy hid the tapes. It was just a delivery boy with their food.

They sat on the floor eating their supper while discussing the tapes. Amy looked across the room and realized she had not hidden all the tapes. The last tape of the discussion with the police about Melissa's accident had not been put away. It wasn't in the same group as the other tapes. They listened to it all the way through only once. It didn't concern them because it had nothing to do with the murders.

112

Amy commented, "I wonder what this tape has to do with the others?"

"I've been wondering that myself. If Mark has been bugging the house, it seems all he has been interested in were the murders. Why keep this one? He doesn't have anything about me complaining to Stephanie about him. He doesn't have any of the conversations Melissa and I had about him behind his back. Wow, when I think of what he knows it gives me the creeps. Every rotten thing I ever said about him was as if I said it right to his face and he never once let on that he knew anything. He's the king of poker face," remarked Ashley.

"Let's listen to it all the way through again more carefully," suggested Amy. "Maybe our answer will be hidden there."

Amy popped the tape in. The tape contained the entire conversation that Karst and Thompson had with Ashley and Stephanie. Ashley began to squirm when she remembered what Thompson had said about Amy.

"That little son of a bitch," exploded Amy. "I hope I do get an opportunity to have him tried in my courtroom. I'll show him just how merciless I can get."

Mark and Kent were on the tape as well.

"I wonder why Mark was questioning Kent so much about what the police had to say about Melissa?" asked Amy puzzled. "I take it he wasn't here when the police were here."

"No, we had a fight, and he left about the same time they arrived," replied Ashley.

"If it was at the same time they arrived, they would've asked him to stay and answer questions," explained Amy.

"Well, he must've left out the back door," responded Ashley.

Amy thought for a moment then implied, "Do you think he was avoiding the police for any reason?"

"I'm not quite sure what you are getting at," admitted Ashley.

"Here listen to this part of the tape again," said Amy.

She rewound the tape to the part where Stephanie was asking about Thompson's inference that Melissa's death may not have been an accident.

"Do you get the impression that Thompson thought it was not an accident after all, but they didn't want to let on to you and Stephanie that it could be something else?" asked Amy.

"I still don't get what you mean," stated Ashley. "Are you trying to suggest that Melissa's death was not an accident? Who could possibly want to harm Melissa, or worse yet kill her? I think you're way off base here Amy."

"Oh come on, just go with it a minute," started Amy. "Suppose someone did want to kill Melissa. She spent the entire day here at your house, right? Then when she left to drive home her brakes gave out and she had her fatal accident. The police said there was no brake fluid in her car. That means she arrived here okay, pulled into your driveway, used her brakes, and they worked fine. If you listen to Mark on the tape he asked Kent more than once if the police found anything in the driveway. Kent told Mark no. He said he was listening to the police through the window near the carport. He opened it to spy on the police."

"So, I still don't follow," responded Ashley.

"Don't you think if her brakes were leaking and she spent the day here that pressing the brakes when she came would've caused a spot on the concrete? Mark was checking to see if the police found any brake fluid in your driveway. Kent told him they didn't," explained Amy. "That means the brakes were probably tampered with while her car was still in your driveway. When she began to use her brakes on her way home, the fluid starting leaking out with each pump of the brake until there was no fluid left."

"Well there was no one here that would've tampered with Melissa's brakes. We live in a pretty safe neighborhood. That's what I told the police." Ashley paused, "No one in this house would know how to tamper with brakes, except Mark, and he was with us most of the evening. Besides, why would Mark want to harm Melissa?" asked Ashley.

"My guess is he didn't care too much for Melissa if Mark heard all of the conversations you two were having

about him. Don't forget, Melissa kept pushing you to
divorce him. According to you, she complained a lot about
Mark and his kids. Maybe he had all he could take.
Maybe he slipped out unnoticed and did something to her
brake line," insisted Amy.

"What could he have done to her brake line?"
asked Ashley.

"How the hell would I know, I'm no damn
mechanic. This is all just theory, but I think it's worth
thinking about," commented Amy.

"You really think Mark could've done this don't
you?" asked Ashley.

"Yep, I sure do. I need to get going. We'll talk more
tomorrow when we tell the others. Are you going to be
okay here? Where are Nathan and Arianna?" asked Amy.

"They're at a ball game. They should be home
soon. I'll be okay. I'll see ya tomorrow," answered Ashley.

The next day Ashley went back to Amy's house to
make their second conference call. She felt it was better
to make it from Amy's house than her own. She didn't
want to take any chance of Carol overhearing the
conversation. Too much eavesdropping had already taken
place.

The call was placed and the four of them greeted
each other.

"Did any of you sleep last night?" asked Susan. "I
know I sure didn't."

116

"Me either," yawned Stephanie at the thought of her missed sleep.

"My guess is no one got much sleep last night," stated Amy.

"So what have we come up with so far?" asked Stephanie.

"Tell them your theory, Amy," encouraged Ashley.

"I think it's more than a theory. I think it's a strong possibility," replied Amy.

"Somebody tell us something," demanded Stephanie.

"Well," began Amy, "We went back to Ashley's, copied Mark's tapes and put them back in place. We unpacked his things from the boxes and tried to put them back in a way he might not suspect we were there. Later we listened again to all the tapes. He did focus on us and the murders and all of our conversations about them at the Christmas parties. Nothing else was on the tapes. Then we listened again to the tape of the police interviewing Ashley and Stephanie after Melissa's death. On that tape was Mark himself giving Kent the third degree about what the police found out..."

"So what's your theory?" Stephanie butted in impatiently.

"My theory is that Mark tampered with Melissa's brakes right here in the yard while everyone was in the house. I think Mark killed Melissa," insisted Amy.

"Don't you think you are jumping to conclusions a bit too early," questioned Susan. "I mean, why would Mark want to kill Melissa?"

"Mark hated Melissa and Melissa hated Mark," admitted Ashley.

"Now we know that Mark had the house bugged. He knew that Ashley and Melissa had been talking about Ashley leaving Mark. Melissa kept trying to talk her into it and Mark knew it. My guess is he had enough and wanted her out of his life," said Amy.

"That's pretty drastic measures. I don't think that's enough motive for murder," commented Susan. "There has to be more to it than that. She had to have some information or something that would really push him over the edge. What has Mark ever done that he would be so worried about? From what you guys are telling me, he and Ashley had long ago given up their marriage. I'm sure if Mark was having an affair, at this point in the relationship, stopping Ashley from finding out would not cause him to kill someone."

Stephanie agreed, "That's right. It would have to be something far more serious than that but what?"

"Ashley, is there any way Melissa knew about those tapes? Or did Mark have reason to believe she knew about those tapes?" asked Amy.

"No, well, I don't know. They were locked in the file cabinet. Melissa did go downstairs to do laundry. She liked the larger washer and dryer downstairs better than the one I use upstairs. I suppose she could've stumbled on to something," replied Ashley.

"Mark was downstairs the day of the Christmas party when you sent Melissa to ask him if he needed anything from the store. Remember you made the comment that Melissa was not herself the rest of the evening?" Stephanie reminded Ashley.

"I also thought it was strange that Mark stayed with all of us the entire evening. That was out of character for him," remembered Ashley.

"That's right, and once Melissa left, he disappeared," said Stephanie.

"Sounds like he was keeping an eye on Melissa to me. Maybe she found out something and wanted to tell Ashley and he wanted to make sure she couldn't," implied Amy.

"I don't know. This whole thing sounds a little too shaky to me. I know we are all upset with Mark about spying on us, and we don't know what he is up to, but accusing him of committing murder is pretty serious stuff," reminded Susan. "I think we should just wait and think this through a little longer before we jump to conclusions again."

"I know, let's drug him and drive him across the country. That should fix things," suggested Amy.

This was the first light-hearted comment made and they all laughed.

"Amy's right. We blew it last time we tried to play detective. Let's sit on it for a while. Besides, no one says it was murder with Melissa. The police think it was an accident," reminded Stephanie.

They agreed.

After they hung up the phone, Ashley returned home. She still had trouble sleeping that night. She tried to sleep in late that morning, but the doorbell rang ruining that plan. The twins had already left for school so Carol answered the door.

Carol knocked softly on Ashley's door as she entered.

"There's a Detective Karst downstairs and he'd like to speak with you, Mrs. Wilson," announced Carol.

"I'll be right down," answered Ashley with a trembling voice. How could she possibly hide her thoughts and accusations from Detective Karst?

Chapter 7

Reaching out her hand to greet him she said, "Good morning, Detective Karst."

"Good morning, Mrs. Wilson," responded Karst, "I'm sorry to wake you."

Ashley turned to Carol and asked, "Carol, could you bring some coffee in to us please?"

"Sure," replied Carol as she went to the kitchen to retrieve the coffee.

"Won't you sit down," insisted Ashley as she pointed to an overstuffed chair across from the sofa.

Ashley sat on the sofa and kept the lights dim. She hoped if she was not too close to Detective Karst he might not be able to study her face as intently.

"Thank you," replied Karst as he sat down. "I have a couple more questions for you and I would also like to speak to your husband, if he is at home this morning."

"This morning is not a good time for me, Detective Karst," lied Ashley. "Would it be alright if I met you in your office, at say, eleven o'clock?"

"Of course, I'm sorry, I guess I should've called first. That'll be fine I'll look forward to visiting with you at eleven. Do you need directions to the station?" he asked.

"No, I'm sure I can find it by myself," she said as she rose from the sofa to say good-bye.

Detective Karst was surprised by her rushed attitude.

"Is your husband home? May I speak with him?" asked Karst.

"No, he's in New York. He lives there and I live here."

"But he was here the night of your Christmas party, is that correct?" inquired Karst, trying to gather some information from Ashley, knowing she did not want to talk now.

"We'll talk at eleven," insisted Ashley as she escorted him to the door.

Carol walked into the room carrying a tray with the coffee. She was confused as to why Detective Karst was leaving so soon without his coffee. Ashley quickly made up some story about an appointment she had forgotten.

Carol thought that was an odd thing for Ashley to say since it was her job to make all of Ashley's appointments.

Ashley watched through the parted draperies as Detective Karst drove away.

She hurried to her room and threw on her clothes.

She grabbed her phone to call Amy.

"Hello," said Amy.

"Amy, this is Ash. Detective Karst was here this morning. I panicked and sent him away. I told him I'd show up at his office at eleven. He asked about Mark being here at the Christmas party and wanted to talk to him. I don't think they have closed the case on Melissa's death."

"Somehow that doesn't surprise me with Karst. Some say he has a sixth sense about these things. And you know most of the time he is right. That's what makes him such a good detective. I'm always comfortable when he's on a case that comes into my courtroom. I know he's done his homework; that makes my job easier. I'm not so comfortable having him snooping around where we're concerned. Be careful what you say to him. Have you thought it through yet?" asked Amy.

"No, that's why I called you. I thought we could meet for coffee somewhere. I told Carol I had an appointment that I had forgotten about and that's why I sent him away. So I'd better have some place to go," she explained.

"There's not much time if you're planning to meet him at eleven. Why don't we meet at that little coffee shop downtown that you like, near the police station. That way

123

you'll be close by to keep your appointment," suggested Amy.

"Great, I'll leave right away," agreed Ashley.

Ashley ran down the stairs, grabbed her coat and keys and headed for the door. "I'll be back after lunch," she called out to Carol.

Amy was waiting for Ashley when she arrived. There were two steaming cups of coffee on the table when Ashley sat down.

Amy began, "You know, I've been thinking. Suppose Mark did kill Melissa. If you tell anything to the police that could connect him to the crime he might blow the whistle on us knowing about the murder plans."

"What could I possibly tell the police that could connect Mark to Melissa's accident?" questioned Ashley.

"First of all, you could put him at the scene. You could inform them that Mark and Melissa didn't get along. The fact that Mark slipped away to avoid questioning will set off alarms as well," Amy pointed out.

"Not really. Maybe Mark didn't know the police were there. Just because Mark and Melissa didn't like each other doesn't give him motive to kill her. You don't like Mark. You don't like men in general. That doesn't mean you're going to kill Mark and every man that crosses your path and upsets you," reminded Ashley.

"I agree, but if Karst is on to something, he's very good at connecting the dots. All I'm trying to say is hold back. Don't give him anything he doesn't ask for. Avoid any questions that could be incriminating by beating around the bush without letting him know you are avoiding his questions," suggested Amy.

"Oh God, I'm not such a good liar. I think I'll have guilty written all over my face and I don't even have anything to be guilty about," sighed Ashley.

"Calm down, you'll be fine. I do have a suggestion for you that I'm not sure you're gonna want to hear."

Ashley took a sip of her coffee. She looked over the top of the cup at Amy and lowered it saying, "What?"

Amy continued, "I think you should call Mark right now and tell him casually that Detective Karst is looking for him and see how he reacts. Ask him how he wants you to handle it. Ask him if you should give Karst his number, or if he is planning to come home to visit any time soon so he can talk to Karst in person."

"Thanks, that's a great idea," moaned Ashley sarcastically. "That's what I really need this morning is to talk to both Mark and Karst while trying to hide information from both of them."

"Look at it this way," Amy pointed out, "you can use Mark for practice before Karst."

Ashley looked at her watch. It was ten-thirty.

"You'd better hurry," pushed Amy, who glanced at her own watch at the same time.

"Not here, let's go out to the car," suggested Ashley.

Amy threw some money on the table. They slipped on their coats and went to Ashley's car.

Ashley hesitated for a moment, and then dialed the number.

When Mark answered Ashley said, "Hi Mark, do you have a minute?"

"Sure, what's up?"

"Detective Karst came to see me this morning. He wants to talk more about Melissa's accident. He also asked to speak with you about it. I told him you live in New York, but then he asked me if you were at the Christmas party that night," stated Ashley with a trembling voice.

"So what did you tell him?" asked Mark trying to hide his concern.

"I told him he caught me at a bad time and I would talk to him later this morning. I thought it would help if I knew what you wanted to do so I could relay that information on to him," commented Ashley more in control now.

Amy flashed her a thumbs up. She was pleased that Ashley was able to regain her composure and work Mark.

"By all means tell him I was at the party. You have to tell him the truth right?" agreed Mark.

"What if he asks me about the relationship you and Melissa had. Should I tell him you two didn't get along?"

Mark was quiet on the other end of the phone for a moment. He was suspecting Ashley had more on her mind than she was telling him.

"Look Ash, don't say anything that is going to make me look bad. Do you understand? I'm getting the impression that you agree with that cop that was with Karst that day at the house. Do you think Melissa was killed? Well do you?" asked Mark angrily.

Ashley gasped. Amy pulled back from the phone. She and Ashley were listening together to Mark's answers. She encouraged Ashley to keep talking.

"I'm not sure what to think," responded Ashley. "Is there something you're not telling me?"

"You do think I had something to do with it, don't you? Just because I didn't like that bitch doesn't mean I killed her," yelled Mark into the phone. "You listen to me and you listen good. You go talk to your Detective Karst and you watch what you say. Do you understand me? You make absolutely sure I come off sounding like Melissa's best friend. I don't want any cop snooping around me. I can guarantee if you make me look guilty you will pay, you and all of your Dolphin friends. Do I make myself perfectly clear?"

"Sure Mark, I understand. I don't want to accuse you of anything. I called you to ask you how you wanted me to handle this. Now I know. Don't worry. I'm sure this is still just routine questioning or something. I'll be careful. I promise," said Ashley.

"Good," grunted Mark as he hung up the phone.

"Whew!" announced Amy. "That is one guilty man! I know that tone of voice."

"Guilty? Do you really think so," asked Ashley.

"Guilty!" insisted Amy. "I deal with this every day in my courtroom. I'd say if he didn't kill her, he has something very big to hide that he doesn't want the police to find."

"So what should I do?" asked Ashley.

"Just do what Mark suggested," answered Amy. "You'll do just fine. You'd better run or you'll be late."

"Can I meet you afterwards for lunch?" begged Ashley.

"Can't, I've got court this afternoon. I need to get going myself. Call me tonight," replied Amy as she was leaving the car.

Ashley stepped out of the car and walked to the police station. She told the officer at the front desk she had an appointment with Detective Karst. He called Detective Karst on the phone.

"He'll be right here," he said.

"Right on time," announced Detective Karst. "Come on back to my office and we'll talk."

Ashley followed Karst through the maze of desks back to his office in the far corner of the room. He escorted her into the room and closed the door behind them.

128

"Can I get you a cup of coffee or tea?" he asked out of politeness.

"No, thanks," replied Ashley nervously.

"Well, Mrs. Wilson, I just had a couple more questions if you don't mind?"

"I'd be happy to help in any way," responded Ashley.

Karst stated, "I think we're about to wrap up Mrs. Rivas' case, but I need to know if anyone borrowed her car that day?"

"No, my car was there, and Stephanie's rental car and Mark's car. There was no need for anyone to borrow Melissa's car," answered Ashley thinking that question was an easy one.

"Okay, did she go anywhere during the day that she needed to drive her car?" asked Karst.

"No, she was there all day," answered Ashley.

"So she didn't run errands or pick up guests or drive anywhere that day?" asked Karst.

"Oh wait, she did run to the store for me. We were out of nutmeg and she grabbed some junk food for the kids. I forgot about that," responded Ashley, nervously trying to explain so she would not look like she was hiding something.

Detective Karst jotted notes in his notebook. Ashley squirmed a bit on her chair.

"About your husband," began Karst, "Mark isn't it?"

"What about him?"

"His name is Mark isn't it?" repeated Karst.

"Oh, yes, I'm sorry. Yes, Mark Wilson," answered Ashley.

"He was at the party that day, wasn't he?"

"Yes, he left once in the afternoon to run an errand, but other than that he was home with us the entire time," answered Ashley.

"By with you the whole day, do you mean actually in the same room with you all day?"

"Well, let me think," Ashley hesitated. She was remembering Mark's angry threat. "Yes, he was very helpful and stayed with us visiting the entire day."

"Did he leave the house for a walk or to take out the trash or anything during the time Mrs. Rivas was at your home?" asked Karst.

"No, Mark doesn't like to take walks and Nathan, my son, it's his job to take out the trash. No, I believe Mark was with us the entire time," responded Ashley knowing that Mark was not with them most of the day only the evening.

"How would you say Mark and Melissa got along?" asked Karst.

"Fine, just fine. They didn't see much of each other with Mark living in New York and all," lied Ashley.

"That's right you stated that Mark lives in New York and you live here. Why is that exactly?"

"Well, we all lived here together when we were first married. I have another home in New York. Mark works for a music company in New York and over the years has had to spend more and more time there. He wanted us to move back to join him, but I didn't want to take the kids out of school and away from their friends. Mark's daughter Isha is married and lives in New York. Mark decided to just move there and he comes home to Denver for visits whenever he can. He used to come for all the holidays and weekends but now he stays behind for some of them to be with Isha," explained Ashley.

"Doesn't that put quite a strain on your marriage?" asked Karst.

"Not really, he was so busy when he was here we didn't spend much time together and it helps me with my writing. I didn't do much writing when Mark was here. I need to be alone in the house to write," admitted Ashley.

"But Melissa was there every day wasn't she?" asked Karst.

"Yes, but she kept to herself while I was writing. She took all my calls and didn't allow anything to interrupt my writing time. It was a good arrangement," commented Ashley.

"Carol must be your replacement for Melissa. Is that right? Did they know each other?" asked Karst.

"Yes, Carol is replacing Melissa and no they didn't't know each other. Detective Karst, did you discover something new about Melissa's accident? I would've thought after three months, the case would be closed."

"I've been away on vacation with my wife. When I came back Mrs. Rivas' file was still on my desk. I just wanted to tie up the loose ends and put closure to the case. If you say she didn't loan anyone her car, and Mark was with you the entire time that should be the last of my questions. Thank you for coming in. I'm sorry if I inconvenienced you in any way. Have a good day," he said as he opened the door for her to leave.

"Why did you want to know about Mark? Were you thinking he was somehow involved with Melissa's accident?"

"No, not really. Mark, to the best of my guesses, would be the only one in the house that would have had enough knowledge about cars to arouse suspicion. Not to insult you, but you and your friends didn't appear to be the type of women that knew your way around under the hood of a car. I just consider every case a homicide until I can prove it's not. Once again, thanks for answering all of my questions."

Ashley could tell he was finished with her and she was anxious to be able to leave. She walked slowly out of his door and back through the maze of desks. Outside on the sidewalk again her pace quickened. She hurried to her car. Once inside she sighed a huge sigh of relief. She sat there for a long time with her head up against the headrest rethinking the conversation between her and

Karst. She was confident that he believed everything she said. She felt much better. She started her car and drove home.

When Ashley arrived home, Carol met her at the door with a list of phone calls that needed to be returned. Ashley didn't feel like dealing with her publisher and handling other book business today, but Carol pushed her. That was her job to keep Ashley on course and she did a good job of it.

The afternoon flew by with all the work, and before long, the kids were home from school. Carol and Ashley finished up the remainder of the work.

Ashley offered to take the kids out for pizza, but they announced they had plans for the night. They both wanted to stay over at their friends' houses. They were all working on details for the spring play. They wanted to work late on their ideas and knew Ashley didn't like to go out after them alone, late at night, so they frequently made plans to stay over with friends if they could not arrange a ride home. They didn't have school for the rest of the week, so Ashley agreed.

They went with her to pick up pizzas, anyway. Ashley bought one for herself and the others she sent with the kids for their evening with their friends.

Ashley called Amy and invited her over for pizza. She too refused saying she had an early morning and lots of briefs to read through. Ashley ate her pizza alone while watching a movie. She took a long hot bath and went to bed.

Ashley's sleep was disturbed by a sound in the house. She sat straight up in bed to listen more carefully. She heard someone in the house. She scanned her memory quickly to see if she could remember whether or not she had set the alarm. She remembered she had. That means one of the kids must be home if the alarm was not going off.

She looked at the clock it was three o'clock in the morning. Something must be wrong, she thought as she grabbed her robe and headed for the door. She went to the twins' rooms and they were empty. She checked the bathrooms then went downstairs. The lights were on in the kitchen. She went in to see why one of them had come home early. There was no one there.

She called out, "Nathan, Arianna."

There was no answer. Now she was getting scared. She thought about the alarm again and reassured herself that she had set it. If the kids weren't home, then it had to be Mark home making the noise. She walked to the basement door and opened it. The lights were on downstairs. It was Mark. He had flown home from New York. She wondered why the rush to get home.

"Mark, is that you?" she called from the top of the stairs.

"Yes, it's me. I'll be right up," his voice sounded angry.

Ashley was afraid he had discovered the invasion of his private space in the basement.

He joined her in the kitchen. She was making two cups of tea and set out some cookies.

"How was your conversation with Detective Karst?" asked Mark.

"Well, hello to you too," teased Ashley, trying to lighten the mood.

"Answer my question," demanded Mark.

"The conversation went fine," replied Ashley. "I was right, it was just routine. He had been on vacation and now that he's back he just wanted to finish Melissa's case so he could close it up."

"What did he ask about me?" questioned Mark.

"Not much. He wanted to know if you were here at the party and if you had been outside that day and how you and Melissa got along."

"Well, what did you tell him?" asked Mark with a very stern accusing voice.

"I just answered his questions. If you want to know if I covered for you, the answer is yes. I lied for you. I told him you and Melissa got along just fine. I told him you were with us the entire day and never left our sight. Isn't that what you wanted me to tell him?" asked Ashley with anger rising in her voice.

"Good," said Mark with a more relaxed voice. "You did good."

"I've been wondering, Mark," she insisted. "Why the panic? What are you trying to hide? You weren't involved in Melissa's accident, were you?"

Mark's eyes glassed over, his nostrils flared. He walked across the room to Ashley and grabbed her by both arms. He glared into her eyes.

"What did you mean by that? What makes you think I'm capable of murder? Are your murder mystery books going to that pretty little head of yours?" he said.

"Mark, let go, you're hurting me," cried Ashley.

Mark released his grip on her and walked away. He went back downstairs to his private haven.

Ashley ran up the stairs back to her room. She called Amy.

When Amy answered the phone Ashley whispered, "Mark's home. He's really angry. He grabbed my arms and hurt me. I'm afraid to be alone with him. Oh, here he comes, bye."

Ashley hung up the phone before Mark burst into her bedroom.

"What's going on?" she asked Mark.

"Who's been snooping around my things?" demanded Mark.

"What are you talking about?" she asked.

"Has Carol been in my work area moving things around? She'd better keep her nose out of my things if she knows what's good for her. If she gets too snoopy she's gonna end up like Melissa. You make sure she knows that," screamed Mark as he left the room.

Ashley crawled back into her bed. She called Amy back. Amy didn't answer her phone. She tried her cell phone. Amy answered.

"He found out someone has been downstairs and he thinks it was Carol. I've never seen him so mad before," whispered Ashley.

"I'm on my way over, I'll be there as soon as I can," Amy reassured her.

"Be careful. Park on the street and let yourself in. Come up to my room. I think he'd be furious if he saw you here. I'll lock us in when you get here," pleaded Ashley.

Amy slipped into the house and up to Ashley's room without Mark noticing. Once inside Ashley's room Ashley locked the door and turned on the television so Mark wouldn't hear them talking.

Ashley told Amy about Mark's threat to Carol. They were more convinced than ever before that Mark had killed Melissa. Ashley sobbed.

Mark came back to Ashley's door. He tried to open it and became even more agitated when he realized she had locked him out.

"Open this door!" he yelled, as he pounded on it.

Amy leaped from the bed and hid in the closet. She showed Ashley her handgun that she brought along and motioned for her to open the door.

Mark burst in. "We need to talk," he screamed.

"About what?" asked Ashley.

"About these," said Mark as he tossed his tapes onto the bed.

Ashley looked at the tapes and pretended to not know what they were, "Why what's on those tapes?"

"Your life and the lives of your friends," he responded.

"I don't understand," lied Ashley.

"If you or if any of your friends should decide you need to tell Karst that you suspect me tampering with Melissa's brakes, I'll give these tapes to the police," he said with a cooler tone to his voice.

Ashley continued to play dumb, "Why, what's on them?"

"Come with me," insisted Mark, as he gathered the tapes from the bed.

He took Ashley downstairs to listen to the tapes. Amy made her way out of the closet and placed herself in view of Mark and Ashley from a darkened spot at the top of the stairs. She wanted to be ready to protect Ashley if Mark became dangerous.

Mark played the slumber party tape for Ashley. Ashley tried to act confused.

"Oh, that. The girls were just helping me work up plots for my books," she explained.

"Funny thing, that was fifteen years ago and not one of your books has any of these plots. But your

138

husband and the rest of the husbands were killed exactly the way you girls planned," reminded Mark.

Next, he played the first Christmas party tape.

"Seems to me you girls had it all figured out. You already knew that your plans were carried through. You accused Theresa of murdering all of the husbands then poor Theresa was accidentally killed before she could kill me, according to your plans," explained Mark.

"That's right," admitted Ashley. "Your wife killed my Michael and all of the rest. She was insane. I'm glad you know. I hated not being able to talk to you about it."

"Ah, but that's where you're wrong, my dear Ashley. Theresa didn't kill anyone. Theresa didn't even know your murder plans had been taped," stated Mark with a tease in his voice.

"What do you mean Theresa didn't know about the plans on the tape? I suppose she just carried through the murders from memory. She was the only one at the party that was not very tipsy that night. She probably remembered everything clearly," commented Ashley.

"My poor, poor Ashley. For a murder mystery writer you're not very creative. Theresa didn't kill anyone," whispered Mark as he stroked Ashley's hair.

Ashley turned sharply to Mark.

"If Theresa didn't commit the murders then who did? We know it was none of us. No one else knew about the plots. No one else was there. Oh my God," cried

Ashley, "It was you wasn't it? You killed all of them didn't you? Just like you killed Melissa."

"Guilty as charged," announced Mark as he took a bow.

"Why? How could you?" demanded Ashley.

"You all knew Theresa. You knew what a bitch she was to live with. I wanted out of my marriage. I couldn't afford a divorce and to start over. When you girls planned the murders, it was my perfect opportunity to get rid of Theresa. It worked. You all believed Theresa was the murderer. She's dead, so end of story," bragged Mark.

"Not quite the end of the story," reminded Ashley. "Now I know the truth. I can still go to the police."

"Yes, you could, but you won't. I have a little insurance policy here with these tapes. Would you really risk the lives of all of your friends to get even with me? No one knows but you and me, and a wife doesn't have to testify against her husband," explained Mark.

"So you're going to keep your mouth shut and you're going to make damn sure no one finds out about Melissa or you're all going down with me. Is that understood?" asked Mark.

Ashley crying nodded her head.

"That's a good little wife, and remember, you're my wife until death do us part," laughed Mark as he walked away.

He gathered his things and left the next day to go back to New York.

Chapter 8

Eventually, ten years passed, and Mark never returned to Denver. Ashley kept her promise to stay away from the police. She dropped her idea of divorcing Mark. She was not sure what he would do. She knew he was capable of murder. She knew he was insane. So they remained married on paper only. They led two entirely separate lives.

Amy told the other Dolphins what she had witnessed that night in Ashley's house. They were shocked and angry but agreed they had to go along with Mark's wishes. He had them trapped. If they went to the police he would take them down with him. Even though Amy witnessed his confession, it would still be their word against his and he had the tapes.

The last ten years were peaceful ones in spite of all that happened. Stephanie remained married to Alex. She retired from her ad agency. Her son Tom stepped in and took over. Kent went on to become a police officer, to fulfill his childhood dream.

Ashley continued to write her books. Arianna and Nathan went away to school. Arianna studied law and Nathan medicine. Ashley was quite proud of her children.

Susan also retired from her practice. She had spent her life dealing with other people's problems. She felt she needed a more uplifting lifestyle now and the freedom to come and go as she pleased. Her relationship with Megan was still estranged. Her daughter Dawn went to Europe to study art. Susan was able to visit her often without the constraints of her psychiatric practice.

Amy eased her hatred of men, and to the surprise of the rest of the Dolphins, began to date on occasion. She was a very respected judge among her colleagues, and feared by those who knew they had to face her in her courtroom.

Aside from the traumatic secret that each of them held, their lives appeared normal to everyone that knew them.

Isha and her husband moved to Denver to be closer to Trystan and Lexi, and to put some distance between them and Mark. Isha, Trystan and Lexi no longer ignored Ashley. Although they did not visit often, nor become close friends, they applauded her for staying married to their dad, Mark. The three of them watched their father go from the loving, doting father of modest means, to a successful businessman that granted them their every wish, to a mean, crass self-centered man that felt the need to control everyone and every situation. He kept a tight watch on their spouses, waiting for them to make a move against one of his kids. He was ready to pounce and destroy them like a mother lioness protecting her cubs; no one would dare try to hurt one of his children. They still loved him dearly, but they all wished they could bring back the father of their youth.

Just before lunch one spring afternoon, the doorbell to Ashley's home rang. Carol was out running errands for Ashley. The working relationship between Ashley and Carol was wonderful. After ten years they were still together. Ashley answered the door.

"Oh my God, Stephanie! What are you doing here?" exclaimed Ashley thrilled to see her old friend standing there.

"I'm hungry. What's for lunch?" laughed Stephanie.

"I'm sure we can rustle something up in the kitchen. Come on in. Now really what are you doing here?" she asked again.

"I'm house hunting. Would you like to help?" asked Stephanie as she followed Ashley to the kitchen.

Ashley set out an assortment of deli meats and cheeses.

Stephanie set the table.

"Who are you house hunting for? You?" questioned Ashley.

"I need to find two houses. One for Alex and me and one for Kent," responded Stephanie while she was biting into her sandwich.

143

"Are you and Alex moving to Denver?"

"Yep," said Stephanie with her mouth full.

"Okay, back up a minute. Stop stuffing your face, and tell me what's going on," pleaded Ashley.

"Alex is retired now and agreed to live anywhere I wanted. Kent accepted a job at the police department here in Denver and I thought it would be nice to come home again. I'll be closer to Kent, you and Amy."

"What about Tom? Won't you miss Tom?" asked Ashley.

"Of course I'll miss Tom, but he won't miss me. It's so hard for me to not get involved at the agency and tell him how to run everything. I can't seem to force myself to stay away. I keep dropping in to see how he's doing. It's putting quite the strain on him. I figured the miles between the agency and me would allow Tom to handle it by himself. I'm only a phone call away, and heaven knows I have the bucks to fly back on a moment's notice. The same goes for him coming for a visit."

"Wait until I tell Amy, she'll be just as thrilled as I am," remarked Ashley with excitement in her voice.

"So are you going house hunting with me or not?"

"Sure, when do you expect to move? How about Kent, when will he get here?" asked Ashley.

"Kent has been here for a few months already. Actually, I'm a little surprised he hasn't paid you a visit by now," replied Stephanie. "We'd like to make the move as soon as I find a house for us. I have an appointment with a realtor later this afternoon."

Ashley and Stephanie drove around the rest of the afternoon, checking out houses with the realtor. Stephanie was thrilled to find a large house for sale not too far from Ashley's house. They chose to look across town for Kent. He already told his mom that if she was going to have to live in the same city, she couldn't live next door. After the way she bugged Tom, he didn't want her telling him how to handle criminals or her watching his every move.

They narrowed the choices for Kent down to three.

"Will he be able to afford one of these on a cop's salary?" asked Ashley as she looked over the paperwork on the three homes.

"Of course not. I'll be buying both of the houses. I bought Tom his last year, so it's only fair I pay for Kent's. Let's see if we can find him and show him these houses."

"This is just your first day of looking. Don't you think you should take a few more days to see what else is out there?" suggested Ashley.

"Nope, if I move in and don't like it, I'll just find another."

Ashley just laughed at Stephanie and her carefree attitude towards life. She envied her. Even though Mark was no longer a part of her life, his hold over her cast a shadow over her that no one else could see.

Stephanie placed a call to the station where Kent worked. "I'm sorry ma'am, Officer Nolan is out on a call. Would you like me to take a message and have him return your call?" asked the voice from the officer answering phones.

"Yes please, this is his mother. Would you have him call me on my cell phone? Thanks."

Kent was a rookie cop and had to take some harassing from the older, more seasoned guys. Across the police radio came the message, "Officer Nolan, your mommy called and wants to talk to you when you get a minute."

Kent was at his first homicide and the excitement of it all was dampened by his embarrassment. The other officers at the scene laughed at him and he wanted to crawl under his cruiser. He tried his best to laugh with them, but he was dying inside.

"She's not even moved here yet and she's interfering with my job," Kent mumbled to himself.

Kent was the first officer at the scene with his partner. The neighbors had called in a complaint about screaming coming from the next apartment. The officers arrived at what they had expected to be a domestic dispute. When they arrived the apartment door was open. Kent and his partner entered with their guns raised and began to look around. They called out to any one that might still be in the apartment. It appeared to be empty.

Just as Kent's partner was about to call it in, Kent noticed lines in the nap of the carpet going from the bed to the closet. He followed the trail, when he opened the closet he found a woman's body concealed under a pile of laundry. Upon first inspection by Kent's partner, the closet appeared to have no one there, just laundry. Obviously, the woman had been killed on the bed and dragged to the closet, where she was covered with the clothes and the attacker fled the scene.

Kent called it in as a homicide and waited for the homicide crew to arrive.

Detective Karst was one of the first on the scene.

"Which one of you guys found the body?" asked Karst.

"That would be me, sir," admitted Kent trying to act professional but being extremely proud of his work.

"Step over here and tell me what you know," stated Karst.

"Well sir, we took the call for a domestic dispute. When we arrived the door was open. We searched the apartment and found no one. I noticed the drag marks on the carpet over there and followed them to the closet. That's when I looked under the clothes and found the body," reported Kent.

"Good work, Nolan, good work," Karst complimented the keen eye of the rookie cop.

After Karst finished writing his notes he looked at Kent again. He studied his face more carefully. Kent was tall, about six one, with dark, tight, curly hair that he kept cut short. He had a muscular build. It was obvious to Karst that Kent worked out. That also made an impression on Karst since he so firmly believed that working out and staying fit makes for a better cop.

"How do I know you?" asked Karst.

Kent was surprised that Karst recognized him after so many years.

"Well sir, you were investigating a car accident at a friend of my mother's and I was just a kid. You were kind to me and told me I'd make a good cop someday and to look you up when I became one."

"So why didn't you look me up then?" asked Karst.

"Well sir, I don't know, sir. I guess I didn't want to bother you sir," replied Kent nervously.

"Relax Nolan, I won't bite. I think you did a good job here. Do you have any interest in becoming a detective?"

"Do I? Yes sir, that's my dream," announced Kent.

"Well keep up the good work and put in your time. I think you can make it happen," encouraged Karst. "Stop by my desk sometime when you're off duty and I'll show ya the daily grind of a detective. It's not always as glamorous as it seems from the outside. You may change your mind."

"Gee thanks, Detective Karst, you can be sure I'm going to take you up on the offer," beamed Kent.

"Oh, and ignore the guys teasing you about your mother. I have a lot of respect for a guy that's close to his mother. It shows a gentle, compassionate side. A good cop is not just a tough guy, but also one that can have empathy for the victims and their families. That's what makes the difference between a good detective and a great detective. So just ignore them," winked Karst as he turned to walk away.

Later that afternoon, when Kent got off duty, he called his mother.

"Hey mom, what's up? I got your message," said Kent.

"Ashley and I found three houses for you to look at. When do you think you can check them out?"

"Not tomorrow, but probably the day after. I'm off duty then," replied Kent. "How long do you think it'll take? I'd like to go by and visit with Detective Karst. I ran into him today and he remembered me from Ashley's house when I was a kid. Can you believe it? He's so cool. He's invited me to his office to show me the ropes about being a detective. I'm so glad I picked Denver to apply for a job. I can't believe it. I'm really excited about this. I think he likes me. If he gives me a recommendation, I stand a stronger chance of making it to detective sooner. At least I hope that's the way it works."

"That's great, Kent, I'm so happy for you. Day after tomorrow is fine. I'll set up an appointment with the realtor and get back to you about the time. Say, would you like to join Ashley and me for dinner tonight?"

At first Kent wanted to decline to make sure his mother didn't expect him to spend all of his time with her while she was here, but then he remembered what Detective Karst said. He decided to go to dinner with the ladies after all. This could begin to be the difference between a good detective and a great one.

"Sure, just tell me when and where to meet you and I'll be there," answered Kent.

Stephanie responded, "Hang on a minute. Ash, where would you like to go to eat tonight?"

"Oh, I don't care, let Kent pick," suggested Ashley.

"Ashley said to let you pick. What sounds good?" asked Stephanie.

"A big juicy steak sounds good. How about Stuart Anderson's?"

"Okay, we'll meet you at the one nearest Ashley's house around seven. See ya then," said Stephanie.

"Bye"

"Hey, I've got an idea," suggested Stephanie. "Let's call Amy and she if she can join us. What do ya think?"

"I'll give her a call. I'm sure she'd like that, as long as she doesn't have a big date tonight," laughed Ashley.

"I still can't believe Amy is actually dating, can you?" laughed Stephanie.

"Shhh," hushed Ashley. "Hi Amy, guess what? Stephanie's in town. Wanna have dinner with us tonight?

We're meeting Kent at seven. We can swing by and pick you up if you'd like."

"Sounds like a plan to me. I'll be ready and waiting. What's Stephanie in town for?" asked Amy.

"That's a surprise. We'll tell you tonight at dinner. See ya later," teased Ashley.

The three girls entered the restaurant. Kent already had a table ready for them. He didn't know Amy would be there. He apologized for being short one place setting. When the waiter came by, Kent had him set another place.

Stephanie beamed while Amy and Ashley made a fuss over Kent.

"Gee Steph, you didn't tell us how good looking he was," teased Amy as she ran her fingers through his short, curly hair.

"Hands off. I liked it better when you were a man hater," joked Stephanie.

Kent, on the other hand, was thrilled to have the attention and he especially liked the fact that his mom's friend, Amy, was such a respected judge. Can't hurt to have friends in high places.

"So tell us about your day," insisted Ashley.

"I thought you'd never ask," joked Kent. He was actually quite the charmer. He was good looking, well mannered and dedicated to his work.

"Today was my first homicide. I was the one that found the body. Some poor woman was killed, probably by her husband or lover. I didn't get the whole story yet. Maybe tomorrow I can check it out when I get to work. I won't go into any details. I'd hate to upset you ladies before dinner arrives."

Stephanie laughed, "I don't think a little murder talk is going to upset these two."

Amy and Ashley looked at each other in shock. They wondered why Stephanie was being so calm connecting them with murders. Surely she hadn't told Kent their secret.

Kent laughed too. "That's right. I guess Amy has her fair share of gruesome details in the courtroom and Ashley writes the gruesome details."

Amy and Ashley relaxed and laughed with them.

Amy remembered Ashley and Stephanie had a surprise for her.

"Hey, what's this big surprise you guys are going to spring on me?"

Stephanie started to answer when the waiter came to take their order.

After they placed their orders Stephanie began again, "Alex and I are moving to Denver. Ashley helped me pick out a house today."

"What? You're kidding. That's great," said Amy.

"Speak for yourself," teased Kent.

Stephanie threw her napkin at him. He threw it back, then flicked water on her from his glass.

Amy said, "You two, control yourselves. I know from experience it doesn't take much to get your mother into a food fight. Keep in mind I'm a prominent judge in this community and I can't be thrown out of a restaurant for having a food fight."

Stephanie and Kent looked at each other and raised their glasses over Amy's head as if they were about to pour water over her head when the waiter returned with their salads. They lowered their glasses and everyone at the table laughed.

The rest of the evening proved to be entertaining.

Two days later Stephanie contacted Kent to make arrangements to show him the houses she had picked for him. He really didn't show much interest. He kept checking his watch. He was anxious for the tours to end. He wanted so badly to get to the station and spend as much time with Detective Karst as he would allow.

"I'll tell you what, Mom, you just pick one for me. I'm sure I can trust your judgment. I like all three. So anything you pick will be great. I really appreciate all that you are doing for me but I should really get down to the station before much more of the day slips away," he said as he kissed Stephanie on the cheek and headed out the door.

Stephanie was left standing there with the realtor.

"Let's draw up the paperwork on the second house. I like that one the best," stated Stephanie.

153

Stephanie spent the rest of the afternoon in the realtor's office signing papers for Kent's house as well as the house for Alex and her. Having the money to spend cash for both homes sped the paperwork up tremendously. Plans were made to close and Alex and Stephanie would make the move the following month.

At the station, Kent nervously asked Officer Dailey behind the front desk for directions to Detective Karst's office. Kent showed him his identification. Instead of calling Detective Karst he just pointed the way.

Kent knocked gently on Detective Karst's door.

"Come in," called Karst.

Kent stepped into the office. Karst was on the phone. Kent sat down to wait. His eyes studied every inch of the office. Karst kept a tidy space. All of his papers were stacked in neat piles. His files were arranged in a file holder on his desk. There was no sign of an ashtray or stacks of used paper cups with coffee stains on them. This was not exactly what Kent had pictured. But he was pleased. Kent was a neat freak himself. He thought Detective Karst was a very organized person. That must be how he handled his cases. He must be very thorough and organized.

"Sorry about that," apologized Karst as he hung up the phone. "What can I do for you?"

At first Kent thought maybe Karst didn't remember who he was or had forgotten he offered an invitation to learn about being a detective.

154

The phone rang again.

"Excuse me a minute," said Karst as he took his call.

Kent began to squirm a little now. Karst was obviously a very busy person. He probably didn't have time for Kent. He felt like he shouldn't have come.

"I'm sorry again," said Karst. "Let's step out of here so we don't get interrupted again. Have you had lunch yet?"

"No, sir. I haven't."

"Great, let's go, my treat," suggested Karst.

Kent couldn't believe his ears. He was about to have lunch with a real detective and not just any detective but Detective Karst.

They walked out of the station and around the corner.

"Here's a great little hamburger joint. Let's slip in here," insisted Karst.

Kent followed him like a lost puppy. Karst could've taken him to eat almost anything and he would've happily agreed to it.

Kent waited for Karst to order and ordered the same. He studied everything Karst did. Karst was soon to become Kent's idol. He wanted to model himself as closely after Karst as possible.

Karst studied Kent as well. He saw the same enthusiasm and spark in Kent that he remembered in himself. How badly he wished he had someone to take him under his wing when he was a rookie. He felt he could do just that for Kent.

"So how long have you been on the force now?" asked Karst.

"Almost two years," answered Kent.

"Where did you start out?"

"Just outside of LA."

"What made you choose Denver?"

"I spent some time here when I was a kid. My mom is originally from here and I kinda like it here. So I thought I would give it a try and..." Kent paused.

"And what?" questioned Karst.

Kent began to blush, "Well, I really want to be a detective and I remembered you said to look you up when I grew up and I thought maybe by some odd chance you could help me. I thought I didn't have anything to lose, so I moved to Denver."

"That's pretty damn flattering, Kent, I'd be happy to do what I can to show you the ropes. Keep in mind, though, you still have to put in your time."

"I know, but anything you could show me I'd appreciate," said Kent.

As they ate their lunch Karst began to teach Kent his philosophy of police work. He told him how he likes to see things done. He explained to him the mistakes he and others have made along the way. He tried to educate Kent in a way that he could learn from the mistakes of others and not have to repeat them himself.

156

Karst didn't have any kids of his own and he saw something in Kent that attracted him. He couldn't quite put his finger on it. He knew he planned to spend a lot of time with him. That sixth sense of his was surfacing again. Karst had learned to go with his feelings and not try to analyze them. Eventually, the purpose would show itself.

Time flew by as Kent pumped Karst about his past cases. Kent was amazed at the details Karst could remember about his cases. He wondered if all the detectives had the same ability and if that was something that he needed to begin developing.

Karst looked at his watch.

"Hey, I've gotta run. It's been a pleasure visiting with you, Kent. Please come by any time you have some free time. I'd be happy to show you a case or two and see what pops up in your mind about them. Who knows, you might find something I've missed," commented Karst as he wiped his mouth with his napkin. He took out his wallet, removed some bills from it, and laid them on the table. He winked at Kent as he left.

Kent watched Karst leave the restaurant and walk down the sidewalk until he was out of sight. He sat at the table alone, sipping on his soda. "Wow," he whispered. "I can't believe today really happened."

Kent went back to his apartment and called his mother. He was curious as to which house he would be living in. Now that he had made friends with Detective Karst, other things in life came back into the picture.

"Hi, Mom," said Kent as Stephanie answered her cell phone.

"Hi Kent. How was your day?"

"Couldn't have been better. Say, where am I going to be living?" he asked.

His mom chuckled, "I wondered when you would begin to wonder. I bought the second house she showed us. Is that okay with you?" asked Stephanie, hoping she'd made the right choice.

"That's great. That's the one I would've chosen," agreed Kent.

"You said you had a good day, what did you do?"

"I told you, Mom, I was going to meet with Detective Karst. Do you remember him? He was at Ashley's house when Melissa died. He was the detective doing the interrogation. Remember how he told me when I grew up to look him up and he would help me? Well he actually remembered me, and he is going to be my mentor. Can you believe it? Isn't that great?" asked Kent with so much enthusiasm in his voice his mother could feel him beaming right through the phone.

"I'm so happy for you, dear. You'll have to tell me all about it when I get back. I'm leaving tomorrow to go back home and start packing. I'll call you when I get there.

Stephanie hung up the phone. She was at Ashley's with Ashley and Amy.

"What's wrong? Doesn't Kent agree with your choice of houses?" asked Amy.

"No, he's fine with the house."

"Then what's wrong?" asked Ashley. "You look upset about something."

"It's probably nothing, but Kent had lunch today with that Detective Karst guy that came here when Melissa died."

"That's probably just part of his job. I'm sure there's nothing to be concerned about. Karst is a detective. He and Kent will cross paths occasionally. It's not like they are going to work together. Besides, Karst doesn't even know there's a connection," said Amy.

"He remembered Kent when he was a boy. He remembered coming here to talk to us about Melissa. He wants to be Kent's mentor," moaned Stephanie.

"Holy shit! Karst keeps coming back like a damn boomerang. That was ten years ago. I hope Kent doesn't bring up Melissa's case and open a can of worms with Karst. I'd hate to have Karst find some lost detail and drag Mark into all of this. Mark wouldn't think twice about exposing us," complained Amy.

Ashley held her stomach as if she were about to be ill. "I don't think I can go through this again. When will it end?" sobbed Ashley.

Chapter 9

Entering the room, Carol brought the mail to
Ashley. Included among all the junk mail and bills were
birthday cards. She had been so busy lately and
emotionally drained over the recent news about Karst that
she forgot her own birthday.

She opened the cards. They were from friends, and
fans. The Dolphins never forgot to send cards to each
other once they re-united some twenty-five years ago.

Ashley dwelled on her life. If she could just put to
rest the haunting secret of the murders and Mark, she
had a good life. Her time with Michael was good. Many
envied her writing career and she had two of the most
wonderful children a woman could ask for. She was
lonely in her self-induced prison. She and Mark had long
given up their marriage. She stayed faithful to that piece
of paper that bound them together. She was afraid to get
a divorce. She remembered his threats. She knew he
would do something terrible if she divorced him. If his

murder of Melissa ever surfaced, she would have to testify against him. He forced her to stay with the marriage to protect him, knowing a wife cannot be forced to testify against her husband.

Ashley was afraid to date, to fall in love, to need a man again. She was afraid once she became emotionally dependent on a man, Mark might kill him as he killed her first husband. The pain of Michael's death was unbearable. No way was she putting herself through that again.

Ashley read through the cards then went back to work at her computer.

"You have mail," came from the speaker on the computer.

Ashley saved her work and checked her email. Usually, she turned down the volume and waited until she finished writing for the day before she checked her email. Today, however, she welcomed the interruptions.

She was hoping to hear from the twins.

Susan had sent Ashley an electronic greeting card. It was a cute cartoon about women getting old and saggy, which made Ashley smile. The note attached said, *Hope your day is a happy one. Be thankful you have your books to keep you company. I'm so bored! Write or call sometime. Love, Susan.*

Ashley was going to send Susan an email in return, but called instead.

"What's going on?" asked Ashley.

161

"Hi, Ash. It's so good to hear your voice. This is such an empty house without the girls. Dawn is enjoying her studies in Europe. I sure do miss her," confided Susan.

"Still haven't heard anything from Megan, huh?" asked Ashley.

"Nope, she's written me out of her life. I just don't know what to do with myself. I spent my entire life swamped with work. Now here I sit, no social life, no hobbies, no man," whined Susan.

"Why not come for a visit? You can help with Stephanie's housewarming party."

"What housewarming party? Where's Stephanie moving to?" questioned Susan.

"Well, there's really not a housewarming party planned, but if you come we can plan one. Four people constitute a party right? She's moving back to Denver. Kent lives here now. Tom's running Stephanie's business, and she's driving him nuts, so she's moving away to give him peace."

"Is everything alright with her and Alex?" asked Susan.

"Oh sure, he's retired too and told her to pick a house anywhere and they could move there. He likes to travel so much, it really doesn't matter to him where he calls home. They're moving in not far from here," reported Ashley.

"Boy, do I envy you. You have Amy near you and now Stephanie. The three of you will have some pretty good times. I guess I'll have to plan more visits. Can't let you have all the fun to yourself," teased Susan.

"I'm not sure how much fun three women pushing sixty can have, but at least we will be together," admitted Ashley. "You know, with Dawn in Europe, and Megan gone, maybe you should consider moving back as well. You could keep your house there if you want to, and buy another one here. It could be interesting."

"Don't tempt me. I'm pretty desperate here," laughed Susan.

"Then just do it. For once in your life, be spontaneous. I can connect you with Stephanie's realtor and you can be living here in a very short time," encouraged Ashley.

"I don't know, don't you think it'd be kind of silly for a bunch of old girlfriends to pack up and move back home for companionship? What does that say for our lives?" remarked Susan.

"Oh God, Susan, stop analyzing everything and just do it. Pack a bag and fly out today. You can take me out for my birthday and tomorrow we can go house hunting for you. Stephanie, as impulsive as she is, picked the first house she looked at. Then, that same week, she found a house for Kent," laughed Ashley.

"Okay, you're on. I'll see you later today," announced Susan as she hung up the phone.

Susan kept her promise and arrived later that day. Ashley called Amy and made plans for all of them to go out to dinner.

The evening began with small talk about the weather, clothes, the kids, and Stephanie and her new plans.

That led the conversation onto Kent and Karst.

"Why didn't you tell me what was going on?" asked Susan disappointedly.

"We didn't think there was any reason to say anything until we knew for certain there was something to worry about, "explained Amy.

"That settles it. I'm moving back. The four of us together can keep ahead of Karst and Mark," insisted Susan.

The next day she and Ashley went house hunting and Susan decided she could be as impulsive as Stephanie. Although she didn't buy the first house she looked at, she bought a house the first day of searching.

Kent spent every extra moment with Karst. He was at Karst's office every morning until he had to be on duty. As soon as he punched the clock to leave he was back at Karst's desk.

He listened carefully to all the calls Karst made. He studied the way he handled people on the other end of the phone. He observed the way Karst handled the people he worked with. He was fair, but firm. He earned the respect of all those he worked with.

164

Karst sent Kent on an errand. Thompson showed up to discuss a case with Karst.

"I see your shadow is missing. Don't you feel a little naked?" joked Thompson.

"Ah, he's a good guy. He really takes his work seriously. I think someday he'll make a good detective. He seems to have an eye for detail. He lacks a little confidence, but that will come in time. I'm actually starting to look forward to seeing him every morning. Sure beats looking at your ugly mug first thing in the morning," teased Karst.

"Yeah, well, just don't let him get in my way. It's tough enough to get work done around here without babysitting some rookie. Make sure you don't include him in any of my cases. I don't want him messing things up for me," complained Thompson.

"What's wrong? Are you afraid he might find something you overlooked?" asked Karst a little annoyed. He felt the need to defend Kent.

"I've got work to do," mumbled Thompson as he left Karst's office with his feathers ruffled.

Later that day Karst was called into his sergeant's office.

"Some of the guys are a little concerned about this Nolan kid hanging around so much. Is he doing his job, or is he here to avoid work?" he asked.

"No sir, Boss, he's a great kid. He stops by here before he punches the clock and then sometimes on his days off. He just wants to learn. I've given him a couple of easy cases to read through. He's not too bad. With each case he seems to gather more clues. He's pretty green when it comes to covering all the bases, but there's just something about him. If you want me to send him away I will," stated Karst, not wanting to cause any friction in his department.

"No, if you think he's okay he can hang around. Just don't let him get in anyone's way. Maybe he'll be your replacement someday," he said.

"Never, I'm gonna live forever. Haven't you heard?" laughed Karst as he walked out of the office.

Back at his desk, Karst felt glad he had this talk with his sergeant. Now he had permission to teach Kent. That meant he could open files for him and turn him loose with them. He was anxious to tell Kent later that day.

That afternoon, when Kent arrived at Karst's office, he told him about his visit earlier in the day with his sergeant.

"Wow, that's great. Since now I'm on the graveyard shift would you mind if I follow you around on some of your cases? If I wouldn't be in the way or anything," asked Kent trying not to beg.

"Those were my exact thoughts. I wasn't sure if you wanted to put in extra hours for free so I'm glad you asked," responded Karst. "Try to find some time to get some sleep. You won't be very sharp if you're only getting a few hours of sleep everyday."

Kent was beaming.

"I've been thinking. How would you like to work on some of my cold case files? You could take your time and read through them on your own and see what you can come up with. I've gathered quite a collection over the years. Don't be discouraged if you don't come up with anything. That's why they're here," reminded Karst.

He removed his keys from his pocket and unlocked the lower right desk drawer.

Kent looked down and saw a few dozen files that were standing neatly in a row. He got down on his knees and ran his fingers though the tabs on the top of the folders. He was reading the names of the victims listed in alphabetical order. He paused to read a few names.

"Can I pick any of these that I want?"

"I'd prefer you let me pick a few for you in the beginning and then you can choose after that. If that's okay with you?" suggested Karst.

"Sure, whatever you say. I'd be happy to look at anything you'd like to share with me. It's been fun going over the cases you already solved to try to solve them too, but this is much more exciting, this is new territory. I mean, maybe I could actually find something that's been overlooked. This is what real detective work is all about."

"Let's set some ground rules," said Karst. "First, you need my permission to get into these files. I have the only key. Second, if you take a file you need to write it down on a log sheet that I'll make up for you. I need the name of the file, and the date you took it out. I want you to sign your name to take it out. And you had better be damn careful not to lose anything that's inside. Also, you cannot under any circumstances go out on your own to investigate anything. Understand? If you have an idea, you come to me with it. We discuss it, and if I think you're on to something, I take it from there. Is all of this perfectly clear?" insisted Karst.

"Yes sir, perfectly clear," confirmed Kent as he rose to his feet.

"And another thing, quit calling me sir. My name is Glen."

"Yes, sir, er I mean, sure Glen, thanks."

Two months past and Kent went with Karst every chance he had. His mother was a little concerned about how much time he spent on the job. She was afraid he left no time for a social life of his own. He'd not had her over to his new house once since he moved into it.

Stephanie made the move to Denver. Alex was off in France for a short while. He preferred not to get involved with that task.

Susan also made her move. She was already enjoying talking with the other Dolphins almost daily and getting together frequently to shop and eat out. She was much happier now.

Kent was working at the office with Karst. They were going over a new case that Karst was working on. It was a hit-and-run pedestrian accident. Karst was allowing Kent to call all the shots. He was watching him every step of the way. He was pleased how well Kent took the initiative to jump right in. He made very few mistakes. He took every detail, as he discovered it, to Karst for approval. Aside from one or two corrections, Kent was going to close this case on his own.

In all his years of being a detective, Karst had not run across anyone with the natural ability Kent had for solving crimes. He was definitely going to be an asset to the force once he made detective, and Karst was going to do everything he could to speed that up.

It was Friday afternoon. Kent pulled together the final details of the hit and run case. It was over. Kent had identified the driver. He and Karst arrested him earlier that day. Karst had not allowed Kent to stop there. He reminded Kent of the tons of paperwork necessary to file the case and then win in court.

"The investigation is the easy part, but you're judged heavily on your paperwork. So you did a good job," praised Karst. "Let's go out and celebrate."

"Sounds good to me," agreed Kent. "This time I'm buying. How about the usual?"

"You're on," said Karst as he grabbed his coat.

Off they went to Karst's favorite spot for cheesecake. Cheesecake and good Kentucky bourbon were two of Karst's biggest vices. Kent made a mental note of that from the beginning. He could go along with the cheesecake habit, but had to stop cold at the bourbon. Kent didn't like to drink.

Early the next morning, Kent was awakened by the sound of the phone.

"Hullo," yawned Kent into the phone.

"Nolan, this is Karst. There's been a plane crash. I'm heading out to the site. Wanna go along?"

"Sure. Where should I meet you?" asked Kent as he was jumping up and down on the floor trying to put his jeans on while on the phone.

"I'll swing by and pick you up. I'm on my way. Meet me out front," instructed Karst.

Kent had Detective Karst and his wife Debbie over for dinner shortly after he moved in. He was trying everything in his power to become part of Karst's life on and off the job. It appeared to be working. Now Karst knew where he lived.

Kent finished dressing, brushed his teeth and grabbed his coat and hat. He started out the door when he remembered his badge was still on his dresser. He ran back to grab it. While he was in his bedroom he heard Karst honking for him out front. He raced through the house, out the door and across the lawn to the street where Karst was parked waiting.

"What's the story?" asked Kent.

"Don't have all the details yet. A private plane went down at the Denver Municipal Golf course. Looks like it was just the pilot, no passengers" stated Karst.

"Did the pilot survive the crash?" quizzed Kent.

"Nope. He didn't make it."

"Did it just happen this morning?"

"I'm not sure. We'll know more when we get to the scene and check out his flight plan," explained Karst.

There were police cars everywhere. The area was taped off. A young officer went up to Karst and said, "This way sir, they told me to show you the way."

Karst and Kent followed the young man through the trees until they reached the spot the plane had gone down. It looked as if the pilot had been aiming for a clearing to try to bring the plane down.

Karst commented, "My guess is the pilot was aware of problems. He must've been conscious and with it enough to plan a landing in that area over there." Karst pointed ahead to the spot where there were no trees.

"Looks like he just missed it," agreed Kent.

The plane, a Saratoga, was severely damaged but was not burned.

"This is good," said Karst. "It's a pain in the ass to piece together a good scenario when a plane's been burned."

Kent kept his mouth shut and followed his mentor.

Karst walked around the entire plane looking for anything that was obvious. Then he went over to the ambulance crew waiting with the body on a stretcher. He pulled back the cover to look at the pilot. Kent looked over his shoulder.

171

"He's a young guy. What a shame," remarked Karst as he replaced the cover.

One of the men handed Karst the pilot's identification.

"Trystan. Trystan Wilson. Here's his address. He has his wife down as next of kin on his emergency identification card. Let's get over there to talk to his wife," said Karst.

Karst turned to talk to Kent, but he was off looking at the body. Kent went over to nearby bushes and vomited.

Karst handed him his handkerchief and asked, "What's up? That's not like you. You've seen plenty of dead bodies before."

"I know this guy," explained Kent, choking on his words. "We played together when we were kids."

"Do you know his wife?" asked Karst.

"No, I haven't seen him for a long time," said Kent.

They arrived at Trystan's house. His wife Sue was inside with her mother and Trystan's two sisters, Lexi and Isha.

Detective Karst introduced both himself and Kent to the family. Lexi and Isha immediately recognized Kent.

Kent took the two girls off to the kitchen to visit with them while Karst talked to Trystan's wife.

"I'm so sorry about Trystan," started Kent. "Have you been able to reach your dad?"

"No, we haven't called him yet. We were hoping somehow this was just a big mistake and that it really wasn't Trystan out there missing. Did you get to see him? Is it really him?" sobbed Isha.

Kent spotted a box of tissues on the counter and handed her one.

"I'm afraid so," responded Kent.

Lexi and Isha grabbed each other and began to sob louder.

"Is there anyone you'd like me to call for you?" offered Kent.

"Can you call Ashley? I guess I'll call my dad," said Lexi.

"I'll drive over and tell Ashley in person, but I can call your dad for you if you'd like," suggested Kent.

Isha gave Kent Mark's phone number in New York. The girls left the room while he made the call.

"Mr. Wilson?" asked Kent when he heard Mark answer the phone.

"Yes," responded Mark.

"Mr. Wilson, this is Officer Nolan from the Denver police. I'm afraid there's been an accident sir. It's your son, Trystan."

"Trystan. What happened to Trystan? Is he alright?" Mark demanded.

Kent paused for a moment. He could feel Mark on the other end of the phone. He could feel the panic in his voice, the helpless feeling a parent has when something has happened to one of your kids and you weren't there to protect him. He could hear his rapid breathing while he waited nervously for a response.

Kent wanted to find the right words.

Mark yelled into the phone, "You said something happened to Trystan. What happened?"

"I'm sorry, Mr. Wilson, Trystan had an accident with his plane. He lost control of it and it went down. I'm sorry sir, but Trystan didn't make it," explained Kent.

"No!" screamed Mark as he hung up the phone.

Kent sensed the pain Mark was feeling. No one should have to be told that one of his loved ones has died. No one should have to feel that kind of pain.

Kent walked into the livingroom to join Karst.

"Thank you for your help at such a difficult time," said Karst. "I'm really sorry Mrs. Wilson."

Karst looked up at Kent and motioned to the door. They left.

Once outside in the car Karst told Kent the details.

"Trystan left early this morning. His wife said he liked to fly to relax himself. She said he was a very good pilot. According to his flight plan, he left Centennial Airport on his way to Yampa Valley Airport in Steamboat Springs. He never made it. He radioed in that he was in trouble. A search party was sent out. They found the plane moments after it went down. Seems he almost made a safe landing but as he was approaching a clearing on the golf course his wheels tagged the top of the trees on

174

the south side of the course and the plane flipped and went down."

"I talked to his sisters. They didn't have anything to add. Their father has been notified and I told them I would tell their stepmother, Ashley," stated Kent.

"That's a good idea. If you know the family, I'll let you handle that. Wait a minute. Ashley Wilson. That's right, Ashley's last name is Wilson," remembered Karst.

"Yes, Ashley and Mark Wilson. That's the house I was visiting when I was a boy and you were investigating the death of her nanny, Melissa," reminded Kent.

"Death sure seems to linger around that woman. I think I'll ride along with you. This will be the third time I've been there, no, the fourth," remembered Karst.

Together they drove to Ashley's home. Kent called his mother, Stephanie, on the way and suggested she meet them there. Karst and Kent waited in the car until they saw Stephanie pull up.

Kent went up to his mother. She put her arms around him. He held her. She cried, "Does Ashley know yet?"

"No, not yet, we were waiting for you," replied Kent.

Together they walked to the door. Carol answered the door.

"We need to speak to Ashley," Stephanie told her.

Carol went to get Ashley. Stephanie led the men into the living room.

Ashley looked at Stephanie, then Kent, finally Detective Karst.

"What?" she asked with a trembling voice.

"Trystan was killed in a plane accident this morning," reported Stephanie. She wanted to get right to the point so Ashley wouldn't jump to the wrong conclusion with Karst there and say something she shouldn't.

Ashley was both relieved and upset. She was grateful it wasn't about one of her kids, but still felt badly about Trystan being killed. They were just beginning to get to know each other again.

The two men answered questions for the women and Karst got up to leave.

"I think I'll stay here if you don't mind," insisted Kent as he walked Karst to the door. "I'll see you on Monday."

"I suppose someone should call Mark," stated Ashley, not looking forward to talking to him again after all of these years.

"He's been notified," Kent told her.

Monday morning, when Kent arrived at Karst's office, Karst was waiting for him. He ushered him in and told him to sit down. He closed the door. "Check this out," said Karst as he tossed a file in front of Kent.

Kent looked up at Karst, confused, then reached for the file. He read through it. He looked up at Karst.

"From what I'm reading here, this was no accident. Trystan was murdered," stated Kent with shock in his voice.

"Right. That's what it looks like to me. How can it be anything other than murder when plastic baggies were found inside each fuel tank? According to our guys in the lab, there were traces of jet fuel mixed in with the plane's normal fuel. Their guess is the baggies contained a mixture of air and jet fuel. When the plane rose to, say, above eight thousand feet, the baggies burst sending the jet fuel into the fuel tank. Jet fuel is heavier so it sank. Once it got pumped into the engine, the engine died, rendering the plane helpless. Trystan was trying to land in the clearing but didn't make it. Someone killed that guy."

Kent sat there for a moment, soaking it all in.

"Are you okay?" asked Karst.

"Uh, yeah. I'm okay. Just a little surprised."

"I'd like you to work on this one with me. Is that okay with you?"

"Sure, but I don't know how I can help. I mean I don't know anything. I barely knew Trystan," commented Kent.

"That's okay. You know the family. That gives us a foot in the door. You're planning to attend the funeral aren't you?"

"I guess. Why?" questioned Kent.

"Because I'm going to be your guest there," stated Karst.

Mark arrived in Denver on Saturday night and stayed at Ashley's house. He stayed in Trystan's old room. He never said a word to Ashley. He and his daughters, along with Sue, handled everything for the service.

Tuesday morning was Trystan's funeral. Karst attended with Kent. They sat with Stephanie, Amy and Ashley.

Karst studied all the people that attended. He took Kent aside occasionally, to ask who someone was. Kent in turn checked with his mother.

At the graveside, when all the people were about to leave, the minister went up to Mark and his girls to offer his condolences one last time. He handed Mark a brown padded envelope.

"This came to the church by messenger as we were about to leave for the cemetery. It's for you," he said as he turned and walked away.

Mark slipped it into his coat pocket and went to the car.

Later, at Ashley's house, people gathered for a meal and to visit, as is customary after a funeral.

Mark locked himself in Trystan's room. He stayed there the remainder of the day, the night and the following day. Carol took trays of food to him, but he barely ate anything. Isha and Lexi tried to comfort him, but he just wanted to be alone.

He walked around Trystan's room, picking up different objects to hold them, and run his fingers over them, as if it could bring Trystan back to him in some way.

As he walked past Trystan's desk, he spotted the envelope that the pastor had given him. He opened it. Inside was a cassette tape. He put it into Trystan's tape player. He pressed the play button.

Theresa's voice came out of the speakers; Theresa's voice telling the others how she planned to kill Mark with a remote control plane.

Mark looked around the room quickly to be sure no one else was there. He removed the tape and tore out the ribbon. He sank to the floor; sweat began to bead on his brow, and his heart began to race.

Chapter 10

Nervously, Mark stood up and paced. He needed to figure out what was going on. He whispered to himself, "Why did someone send me this tape? It had to be someone that knew I would be at Trystan's funeral. What does it mean? What does Theresa's plan to kill me have to do with Trystan's funeral? Why not the whole tape?"

Mark walked over to the tape, rewound the mess of ribbon back onto the reel, and checked to be sure there was nothing else on it. He was furious now. It had to be Ashley, he thought. He raced down the stairs to find her. She was in the kitchen visiting with Carol.

Carol looked up at Mark and decided to excuse herself from the room.

Mark grabbed Ashley by her arms. He pulled her close to him so her face was near his.

"How could you do this? What did Trystan ever do to you? This is not the end of it. You're going to pay for this," he exploded.

Ashley squirmed away from his grip and said, "What are you talking about? I never did anything to

Trystan. Are you blaming me for Trystan's death? You've got to be insane."

He grabbed her once again and dragged her out of the kitchen to the stairs. He shoved her ahead. She climbed the stairs to the hall. At the end of the hall he grabbed her again and pulled her into Trystan's room.

Carol watched from downstairs. She went to the phone and called Amy.

Once inside Trystan's room Mark played the tape for Ashley.

Ashley was confused, "What? I don't get it. Why are you playing the tape for me?"

"Someone gave this tape to the pastor at Trystan's funeral to give to me. Only the part about Theresa killing me with a plane is on it. Don't you see a plane killed Trystan. Only you and I know about the tape, unless you told the other Dolphins about it," screamed Mark.

"Hold on a minute," insisted Ashley. "No one said Trystan was killed. It was an accident. I don't know who sent this tape to you, but it wasn't me. You are the murderer in the family, not me!"

With that, Ashley turned and stormed out of the room. At the base of the stairs Carol was waiting to tell her that she had tried to reach Amy but failed. Stephanie would be coming over.

"Thanks, Carol, but I'm fine. Mark has quite a temper but he has never physically hurt me. He's pretty upset about his son dying," explained Ashley.

Stephanie arrived at about the same time as Kent and Detective Karst. Carol let the three of them in. Ashley was right behind Carol.

"Hi Steph, what's going on?" asked Ashley.

"I'm not sure, I met these two when I pulled up. What's up, Kent?" quizzed Stephanie.

"We need to talk to Mark, is he still here?" asked Kent in a stern, business-like tone.

Ashley and Stephanie searched each other's faces for an answer.

"Carol, would you go tell Mark he has company," suggested Ashley.

Carol returned to the living room with Mark.

"What can I help you gentlemen with?" asked Mark in a charming sort of way.

"Mr. Wilson, I'm Detective Karst, and you know Officer Nolan. We need to ask you some routine questions about your son. It seems his accident wasn't exactly an accident. Do you know of anyone that would want to harm him?"

Ashley gasped. Stephanie covered her mouth with her hand. Mark looked across the room at both of them.

"How do you know someone killed him and it wasn't just an accident?" Mark asked.

"Well," began Karst, "our guys at the scene discovered plastic baggies in the fuel tanks of his plane. Someone had to put them there. They contained jet fuel and were probably inflated with air. When they exploded

182

they caused the engines to die. I won't go into any more of the details, but this looks very deliberate. We need to know if he had any enemies?"

"No, not that I'm aware of," answered Mark.

"Can you tell us anything about his relationship with his wife?"

"I live in New York. I don't spend a great deal of time around Trystan anymore. I guess he and Sue were getting along fine. He would've told me, or one of his sisters, if there were a problem. Trystan and his sisters are very close. I mean, were very close.

"How about someone he worked with?"

"Nope, can't help you there either. Sorry."

Karst noticed that Mark didn't appear to be shocked by the news, nor did Ashley. Their reactions were not what he expected. He asked Mark for the phone numbers and addresses of his girls and he left with Kent.

"What's your take on all of this?" Karst asked Kent.

"What do you mean?"

Karst realized Kent was too green to have picked up on the reactions of the family involved. He dropped it for now. They drove to Isha's house.

Karst repeated the line of questions for Isha and she was so shocked she could barely answer. She couldn't believe anyone would want to hurt her brother.

Later they found Lexi and her reaction was nearly identical to Isha's. Their reactions were more normal, thought Karst. He wondered what Mark and Ashley were

183

hiding. Surely Mark wouldn't have killed his own son, or be covering for Ashley if she were guilty.

Karst and Kent drove to the airport where Trystan kept his plane.

They split up and began questioning everyone there to find someone that might have been there on the day Trystan took his plane out.

Kent flagged Karst to come to him. He was visiting with a mechanic that was working on a plane for one of the owners.

"I was just busy working on that plane right over there," said the mechanic pointing to a bright yellow and red Piper Cub. "It was pretty quiet week, only a few people in and out while I was here. I don't know everyone here but I recognize a lot of faces from working on so many of the planes here. I didn't see anything unusual. There were a few women and some men visiting that I didn't recognize but nothing sticks out as being wrong. Sorry I can't help."

"Women and men that you didn't recognize...did they all arrive together?" asked Karst.

"Nope, they came at different times. Some were with people that I recognized. They were wandering around looking at the planes. That happens a lot out here. There's not much security here, not enough money for that. I suppose anyone could come here any time day or night and not be noticed."

"Sometimes people just come with their kids to watch the planes come and go and hope a pilot will show his plane to one of the kids."

"Thanks for your help if you think of anything please give us a call," suggested Karst as he handed him his card.

"That was a waste of time," whined Kent.

"No part of an investigation is a waste of time," corrected Karst. "I want you to come back here and go through the flight plans and see who flew this week and visit with each one of them. If you find anything you call me immediately."

Back at Ashley's house, Ashley sent Carol on an errand. Mark, Ashley and Stephanie were left alone to discuss this.

"Okay Mark, it's no secret that the rest of the girls know about your tape from the slumber party. It involved each one of us so I told them that you had the tape. They all know you killed our husbands, not Theresa. They know you killed Theresa. We all agreed to play your little game to protect ourselves. Why would any of us want to jeopardize our lives now by harming Trystan? If we were going to throw our lives away by committing murder, my guess is, it would've been you we killed, not Trystan."

Stephanie went into the kitchen and came out with a package of chips. She needed to eat when she was nervous. She watched Mark and Ashley pace.

"Someone knows something and that someone killed Trystan," Mark pointed out. "If it wasn't me, or any of you then who was it, and why?"

Stephanie added, "Maybe Trystan had an enemy of his own that none of us know about. It doesn't have to be connected to us, does it?"

"The fact that the tape was given to Mark means someone connected to us had to kill Trystan. Whoever it is wants Mark to know that," insisted Ashley.

Kent exhausted all his options with his interviews. He went back to the office to visit with Karst.

"Nothing, absolutely nothing, I couldn't find one lead. No one saw anything. Not many of them even knew who Trystan was. Maybe you should've handled it," moaned Kent feeling like a failure.

"Just because no one saw anything doesn't mean you did anything wrong," insisted Karst trying to make Kent feel better. "Now, I need detailed reports, pronto. Do it while it's fresh in your mind."

"I know, but I keep thinking I missed something," commented Kent.

"Sometimes when you write it down, you'll remember something that you thought you missed. This one is going to be tough. Go back to the airport and find out how hard it is to get jet fuel. We know the plastic baggies and air can't help us," suggested Karst.

The investigation continued and Mark left to return to New York.

Mark entered the house feeling lonely. Although he and Ashley no longer got along he felt the need now to be with someone that he could discuss this with, someone who shared his secrets.

Mark put his bags in his room and went to the kitchen for a glass of juice. He picked up the phone and pushed the buttons for his voice mail to listen to the messages. *You have 15 new messages,* came the recorded voice from the phone.

One by one Mark played his messages. The fourth message caused him to drop his juice on the carpet. Theresa's voice once again describing her plans for Mark's death came from the phone.

Back at Ashley's all of the girls were together trying to figure out what was going on.

Susan said, "You know, it is not entirely impossible that Mark committed this murder himself."

"Now, why would he kill Trystan? He loved Trystan," reminded Ashley.

"Mark's not a sane person. He might even have a multiple personality disorder. He could've blacked out and a separate personality may have killed Trystan. I've had patients with this disorder but none who've been capable of murder. We do know, however, where Mark is concerned, killing comes easy. Look how quickly he disposed of Melissa when he felt threatened by her. You don't suppose Trystan found out somehow what Mark had done to his mother and threatened to expose him do you?" questioned Susan.

"Anything's possible, but Mark seems to be too cool and calculating to not be aware of his actions. I don't believe he had another personality come out and kill his son. I think he was capable of killing Trystan on his own, but I still believe he wouldn't have done it," answered Ashley.

"Mark has gone to great measures to insure no one finds out about the past murders," reminded Stephanie. "I agree with Susan. If Trystan was going to expose him I think he could do it."

"Remember, the police have no idea when the plastic bags were placed in the fuel tanks. Mark could've easily flown in, placed the bags and taken the next flight home. He could've done it days before the accident. Being in New York gives him an airtight alibi," commented Amy.

"We need to stop him. This is getting out of hand. If Mark did kill his own son, none of us are safe any more. Not that we were safe before this. Mark could decide that we all know too much. He could kill each of us to cover his trail. He's made it this long without being exposed. I think he feels he can do anything now and not get caught. I do catch myself wondering what would've happened to us if we just went to the police in the beginning. Trystan might still be alive if we confessed," insisted Stephanie.

"Stephanie's right, we should've gone to the police years ago when this happened," sighed Ashley.

"Well we didn't do it then and we shouldn't do it now. We still have too much to lose. But I agree with Stephanie, we need to find a way to stop him," commented Amy.

Karst and Kent went out for a bite to eat. During their meal they discussed the case.

"Looks like this one is going to be added to the cold case files if something doesn't break soon," reported Kent.

"Ah, don't give up so soon," encouraged Karst. "We just need to give it a little more time, surely something will show up that can help."

"So," said Karst, "no one saw anyone suspicious at the scene. No one can come up with any enemies that Trystan may have had. There were no fingerprints on the baggies and you yourself found out anyone could siphon a little jet fuel from one of the larger planes to perform the dastardly deed. We have no purchase records to go on. We have no suspects. The only thing out of the ordinary is..." Karst stopped.

"What? What's out of the ordinary?" quizzed Kent excitedly.

"Oh, nothing important, forget it," said Karst. He was remembering the fact that both Ashley and Mark did not seemed surprised by the mention of murder where Trystan was concerned. He didn't want to share that tidbit with Kent. He was too close to the family. He tucked that thought away so he could contemplate it later.

"It might be important, just tell me. I'd like to know," begged Kent.

"I said drop it," responded Karst in a voice that Kent knew to mean he didn't want to be bothered with it any longer.

Kent and Karst ate the rest of their meal in silence.

Karst went home after they ate. Debbie was waiting up for him. He told her about the case and how there were no leads.

Debbie knew her husband well.

"No sleep for you tonight," she said.

"Something just doesn't feel right about Mr. and Mrs. Wilson. I'm not happy with their reaction to Mr. Wilson's son's death," confided Karst.

Karst remembered his comment to Kent about how death seems to linger around Ashley. He didn't like where his thoughts were taking him. He felt maybe Ashley did a little more than just write murder mysteries. Maybe she was one of those messed up artsy types that needed to commit murder in order to write about it. But then, how did Mark fit into all of this? How could he sit back and let her murder his son and protect her? After all, they didn't even share the same house. Their marriage was a joke. Maybe she had something on him. Maybe she had him under her control. Or maybe he was the one in control.

Karst climbed out of bed and went to the phone to call Kent.

Kent answered his phone.

"Nolan," said Karst, "come in a little late tomorrow. I want you to take your mother out to breakfast and find out everything you can about Mr. and Mrs. Wilson's marriage."

"Why? What's up? Are you on to something?" asked Kent.

"We'll talk about it later, just find out every bit of dirty laundry on those two that your mother is willing to give," instructed Karst.

"This is so sweet of you, Kent, we haven't had breakfast together in ages," beamed Stephanie.

Kent was very careful about handling his mother. First he charmed her and won her over during the meal. He made her feel as if she were the best, most appreciated mother in the world. He had such a way of working her when he wanted to; a talent he planned to use on his wife if he ever found one.

"Too bad about Trystan, wasn't it?" began Kent.

"I know, how sad. Have you guys found out anything more about who might've planted those baggies in his plane?"

"Nope, I think we are going to close this case and consider it unsolvable. We have no leads," responded Kent. "How's Ashley these days? Was this very hard on her? How close was she with Trystan?"

"Of course it was hard on her. It was hard on all of us. Trystan was just her stepson, but they had a lot of good memories in the past. Recently they were developing

191

a new relationship after the many years of being separated."

"Why were they separated?" asked Kent.

"Well, there was trouble between Mark and Ashley, and the kids seemed to have taken sides. They used to complain to Ashley when they lived at home with her that they felt Melissa...do you remember their nanny Melissa?"

"Sure, I remember her she died in that car accident. Remember that's how I met Detective Karst the first time," Kent reminded her.

"Of course, well, anyway, the kids felt Melissa didn't like them, so once they went off to college, they didn't come back to spend much time with Ashley. Then, of course, with Mark and Ashley not getting along, Ashley felt the kids thought they would be betraying their dad if they spent time with her," explained Stephanie.

"Why were Mark and Ashley having trouble in their marriage?" asked Kent.

"That's a good question," said Stephanie, scratching her head. "Let's see. When they were first married, Mark was everything Ashley could want in a husband. Actually, Mark was everything any woman could want in a husband. Mark and Ashley had an affair when they were in high school. Mark and his wife, Theresa, were dating in high school. Ashley and Theresa were best friends. Theresa was also part of our group. We called ourselves the Dolphins from a swim team we were all on. Anyway, Mark and Theresa broke up for awhile and Mark and Ashley dated for a time in secret. Then Theresa showed up pregnant and Mark went back to her."

"Later, we all went off to school and Theresa stayed behind to marry Mark. We never kept in touch with her. A number of years later Theresa and Ashley bumped into each other. Now you have to understand, Theresa was a strange character. She could be very, very cruel. All of us walked on eggshells where Theresa was involved, but she was fun to have in our group because she could sure give the teachers a run for their money. Ashley was not sure how Theresa would react to their reunion, since we all sort of deserted her. To Ashley's surprise Theresa was delighted to see her and the two of them planned a slumber party for all of us just like old times."

"We had our little reunion and all of us went back home. Later Ashley's husband died and she was staying with Mark and Theresa. She was pregnant with the twins. Theresa had an accident and was killed. Ashley wanted to help Mark with his three kids and Mark didn't want Ashley to go through her pregnancy alone. They all moved into Ashley's house and things were good. They eventually got married."

"That sounds like a romantic story. Past lovers reunite after many years and fall in love and get married. So what happened to make it go sour?" asked Kent.

"Mark was a teacher and didn't bring home much money. Ashley didn't have to worry about money and could've easily supported all of them and been glad to do it. Mark couldn't deal with it. He was and is a very talented musician. He followed through on a job lead in New York and became very successful. With success came obsession. He stayed away more and more of the time and they just drifted apart. Why the sudden interest?"

"I was just curious. I mean they seemed so happy when I was a kid, and you used to take me there for Christmas once in awhile. I just wondered what happened."

Kent looked at his watch.

"Gotta go," he said as he kissed his mother good-bye. He reached in his pocket for money to pay the bill, but Stephanie refused.

Kent rushed into Karst's office, but he wasn't there. He sat around waiting for him. He noticed the lower file drawer was not completely closed. He looked around to see if Karst was coming before he thumbed through the cold case files. He was very curious about Melissa's death and wondered if he could talk Karst into letting him investigate it a little further. Partly because it wasn't solved, and partly because he was there when it happened. He took the file out and began to look through it.

"Hey Nolan, what are you doing?" demanded Thompson when he walked into the room. He knew he startled Kent and was enjoying it.

"Uh, I'm just waiting for Detective Karst to get back. He sent me on a job this morning and I need to talk to him about it," responded Kent, nervously trying not to look guilty.

"He gave me a message for you in case you showed up while he was gone. He had to go out on a call. He thought you might be interested in. Here's the address. You're supposed to meet him there," said Thompson as he handed Kent a piece of paper.

Kent snatched it from Thompson's hand. He knew Thompson didn't like him, and he didn't care too much for Thompson.

Kent carefully replaced Melissa's file. He almost closed the drawer but thought it would be best to leave it slightly open, just as he found it.

He looked at the address as he was leaving the building. He got into his car and drove across town. There was something familiar about that neighborhood.

In New York, Mark answered a knock at his door. A messenger delivered a package to him. This was pretty common for Mark, as many of his clients sent him CD's to listen to.

He tossed it on his table while he finished his lunch. He wasn't in the mood to listen to a bad song on an empty stomach.

Kent made his way through the crowd of people that had gathered on the street and sidewalks. There was yellow tape all around the yard of what used to be someone's home. Obviously, there had been some sort of explosion.

He watched as two bodies were removed from the remains of the house. He searched the group of men and women on the scene to find Karst. He saw him talking to a uniformed police officer. He went up to him.

He didn't want to interrupt, so he just stood there, looking around and waiting. He looked at Karst, then the remains of the house, then back at the ambulance loading the bodies.

He shot across the debris and climbed over the yellow tape. He stopped the ambulance from leaving and asked to see the bodies. At first, they were going to refuse, but then he flashed his badge.

The driver went to the back doors and knocked. The paramedics inside opened the doors and Kent climbed in. He showed his badge and went to the bodies. He uncovered the first one. It was a man badly burned. Kent did not recognize him.

He went to the next body and unzipped the bag. He saw instantly it was a woman. He studied her charred features a bit closer. He looked over at the paramedics watching him. They continued watching as he appeared to become ill.

One of them put his hand on his shoulder and said, "Hey, buddy are you okay?"

Kent turned to him and said, "I'm not sure, I think I know this woman. Do you have I.D. for her?"

"You'll have to check with whoever's in charge out there. Are you sure you're okay? We need to get going," he said.

Kent climbed down. The doors were closed and the ambulance drove away. Kent went to his car and leaned up against it. He looked as though he was about to vomit. Karst walked over to him.

"Are you okay, Nolan?" he asked. "We need to talk. Let me get things wrapped up around here then let's sit in my car and have a chat. We have to plan our strategy. I really need you to hold together on this one. Can I have someone get something for you?"

Kent shook his head, "I'll be fine," he mumbled.

Mark finished his lunch. He made a couple of phone calls then opened his package. It was just as he suspected, a new CD to listen to. He looked inside the package for a letter to go along with it but found none. He checked the return address but again there was none.

"Great," he groaned, "another idiot so excited to get his music to me he forgot to let me know how to reach him."

At first Mark wasn't even going to bother to listen to it but changed his mind.

He popped the CD in and dropped down on his sofa to listen. He closed his eyes and heard Stephanie's voice planning Richard's death. An explosion was to kill Richard and that is exactly how Mark killed him.

Chapter 11

Leaping to his feet, Mark went to the phone and called the messenger service he most often used. They had no record of the delivery made that morning. He walked around the room, running his fingers through his hair. He was frightened.

"What does it mean?" he said aloud. "Why Richard's death? Is Stephanie involved? Is she trying to drive me nuts? As soon as she found out about Trystan's death, she's probably the one that sent that first tape to me. She's trying to scare me, but why? Is this her way of getting even with me for Richard's death? Why now, after all these years?"

Mark's thoughts changed from Stephanie to the recording. He wondered if this was some kind of threat. Was his life in danger? After all, the girls did say after Trystan's death, if they really wanted to kill someone it would be Mark. Now, he knew how the girls felt, always looking over their shoulder wondering who would be next.

The panic they must've felt. How badly they must've wanted to go to the police, but couldn't. Mark was now in the same situation. The police already knew someone killed Trystan. Mark's hands were tied. He could not blame the Dolphins or they would blow the whistle on him. Even with his life being in possible danger, he could not tell the police.

Later that morning, the phone rang. Mark did not answer it. He listened to the message first. "Mr. Wilson, this is Officer Nolan, I need to speak with you sir..."

Mark snatched the phone up.

"Go on, this is Mr. Wilson," answered Mark.

"Mr. Wilson, I'm not quite sure how to tell you but there has been another accident. I'm afraid your daughter Isha and her husband were involved," Kent paused for a response before continuing.

"Is she okay?" questioned Mark.

Kent could hear the sadness in Mark's voice accompanied by anxiety.

"I'm afraid both she and her husband died instantly," reported Kent.

Mark sank down on the sofa. He wanted to sob but controlled himself.

"Was it...was it, an explosion of some type?" asked Mark with a trembling voice.

There was a long pause on the other end of the phone.

Once again Kent, could feel all the emotions that were filling Mark's body. He could hear his rapid breathing, the tremble in his voice, the pain he must be suffering having lost two of his children so close together.

"How did you...I mean, yes, it was an explosion," reported Kent.

"I'll catch the next plane back," mumbled Mark as he hung up the phone.

Karst walked over to his car. Kent was waiting for him inside.

"How ya doing? Any better?" asked Karst sympathetically.

"Man, when you know the deceased, it really hits you hard. You handle the death of strangers so well. I guess that's not all bad. Remember I like a sensitive cop. It's way too easy to become hardened in this line of work."

"I'm sorry. I don't mean to come off as such a wimp. I don't know why it hits me so hard," apologized Kent. "It's not very professional. I'll try harder next time."

"Hey, let's hope there's not a next time. Two are plenty. I guess we have some calls and visits to make. Are you up to it?" questioned Karst.

"Yeah, I can pull myself together. I already put a call into Mr. Wilson while I was waiting for you," replied Kent.

"How'd you manage that? Where did you get his number?" quizzed Karst surprised.

"I had it in my notebook. Isha gave it to me when Trystan died. I'm the one that made the call to Mr. Wilson that day. The girls weren't feeling up to it," explained Kent.

"Good work Nolan. See, even under these circumstances, you are still able to keep your wits about you and go to work. What was his reaction?" asked Karst curious because of the reaction he got out of Mark when he told him Trystan was murdered.

"He was pretty upset," responded Kent, "but...he, well..."

"Well what? Spit it out, Kent," pressed Karst.

"It's probably nothing, but he asked me if they died in an explosion. I don't remember telling him it was an explosion. But then as shaken up as I was maybe I did and just didn't remember," remarked Kent.

"You're right that's a bit odd. Unless the guy is psychic or someone else had already called him," commented Karst, not wanting to point blame to Mark just yet.

He needed Kent to be honest and open with the family, without having to hide the idea that they may think Mark was involved.

"Let's take a ride over to Mrs. Wilson's and tell her before Mr. Wilson has an opportunity to," suggested Karst.

"Why Mrs. Wilson? Shouldn't we go to Isha's sister Lexi next?" questioned Kent, confused about the order in which Karst chose to inform the family.

"Maybe she should hear it from a family member. Maybe her dad or Ashley will call her. Of course, we will do it for them if they want us to," stated Karst trying to cover his tracks.

They drove directly to Ashley's. As they pulled into the driveway, Ashley was backing her car out from behind the house. She looked out her side window and saw them. She stopped the car and the two men approached the driver's side window.

Ashley lowered the window.

"Can I help you gentlemen," she asked.

"We need to visit with you, could you step inside the house a moment?" asked Karst. He wanted her out of the car where he could watch her and study her body language.

Ashley stepped out of the car and the two men followed her to the back door of the house. They stepped inside to the kitchen.

Ashley sat at the table and waited nervously for what ever they had to say to her.

Karst noticed that she was nervous. She started out sitting still with her hands in her lap. Then she reached for the cloth napkin on the table and began to play with it while she watched them.

"I'm sorry to report Mrs. Wilson, there's been another accident," started Karst.

Ashley sat perfectly still. She looked from one man to the other without saying a word. She was trying to read their faces. She was trembling inside hoping it was not about one of her kids.

Karst continued, "I'm afraid your stepdaughter Isha and her husband were killed this morning in an explosion in their home."

Ashley's shoulders lowered. The tension left her face. She took a deep breath.

"Has anyone notified their father yet?" she asked.

"I called him," responded Kent.

"How was he? I mean how did he take the news?" she asked.

"Not well," reported Kent.

Karst continued to study Ashley. He was confused. She was obviously worried about something, then relieved, then curious about Mark. She did not cry or ask any questions.

"Poor Mark," she said. "I'm not sure how he is going to cope with the loss of two of his children."

"Is there anything else?" asked Ashley.

"No, that is about it for now, Mrs. Wilson," replied Karst.

Ashley walked out with the two of them, returned to her car and drove away.

Karst and Kent returned to their car.

"Wow, that's one cold woman. She was totally void of any emotion. Did she and Isha not get along?" Karst asked Kent.

"She was a bit strange, wouldn't you say," agreed Kent. "I was under the impression that her stepkids were beginning to renew their friendship with her after a number of years being out of touch."

Karst started his car and drove in the direction Ashley had disappeared down the street. He caught sight of her up ahead but did not let on to Kent that he was following her. She pulled into a driveway, leaped out of the car and ran to the door.

As they passed the house that she ran inside Kent made the comment, "See that house right there? That's my mom's new house."

Karst now knew that Ashley was with Stephanie. He had to wonder if they were involved in this together. He felt sure by Ashley's reaction again that she was not without some type of guilt.

Karst wasn't sure yet if Isha's death was by accident or planned. He did know that Ashley acted suspiciously and Mark seemed to already know it was an explosion. What was going on here?

"Let's head back to the office and see what's come in on this case for the cause of the explosion," suggested Karst.

Karst sat at his desk reading messages. Kent sat in the chair across from his desk fidgeting.

"Hey, can I go through your cold case files while we wait for the report to come in?" asked Kent.

"Geez Kent, don't we have enough to work on already?" remarked Karst as he reached in his pocket for the key to unlock his drawer.

Kent went to the drawer and thumbed through the files for a moment. He pulled out Melissa's file. He laid it out on a portion of Karst's desk, being careful not to encroach on Karst's space. This was not a difficult task; Karst had the cleanest desk in the building.

Kent read through everything carefully. There just wasn't much there. He noticed that evidence was inconclusive about whether or not Melissa's car had been tampered with. That must be why Karst kept the file instead of considering it case closed.

"Why are you keeping this case open? I mean, why didn't you think this was just an accident pure and simple?" asked Kent.

"Let's see, what are you looking at?" questioned Karst as he reached for the file turning it around so he could read it.

Kent got up and stood over his shoulder.

"To be honest with you, I don't know. I guess it was just one of those gut feelings. I have no reason to believe it was not an accident, but something about it keeps haunting me. You know, if you take this case and add it to the two recent deaths that draws Mrs. Wilson into all of them."

Kent responded, "Whoa, you don't think Mrs. Wilson is somehow connected to the murders do you?"

Karst was not sure he really wanted to bring Kent into this, but decided he was a pretty sharp rookie and maybe if he did have some seed of doubt planted he could find something that may have been overlooked.

"I'm sorry but I have a hard time thinking Ashley could be involved. I would be more apt to think Mark would be," replied Kent.

Karst looked across his desk at Kent who had returned to his chair.

He raised his eyebrow and said, "What makes you blame Mr. Wilson over Mrs. Wilson? After all it was Mr. Wilson's kids who just died."

"Well, first of all we don't know that Isha's death wasn't an accident. We know that Trystan was murdered but we have no clues. It could've been a random act of violence. It could've been anyone's plane, but it just happened to be Trystan's.

"About Melissa, from what my mother told me, Ashley thought the world of Melissa and went into a state of depression when she died. That just doesn't sound like anyone who is capable of these murders," insisted Kent.

"Maybe you're right, but she's still hiding something. I have to follow my instincts," commented Karst.

Before their conversation could go any further the report they were waiting for was delivered to Karst's desk. He looked it over and handed it to Kent.

"Nothing," said Kent. "Their furnace caused the explosion. There must've been a gas leak."

"Let's go see if we can find out anything about the condition of the furnace before the explosion," suggested Karst, as he stood up and pushed in his chair.

"How are we going to find out that?" questioned Kent.

"I'm not quite sure. Maybe we can find out who sold the house to them and see when the last inspection was done. Maybe we'll have to call every heating and air-conditioning service in the phone book. I need to know what caused the explosion," responded Karst.

Kent followed Karst. He drove back to Isha's neighborhood. He drove up and down the streets, writing down the names and numbers of any real estate companies that had signs on lawns. He pulled over to the side of the road.

He called the first one. He explained who he was, gave them Isha's address and asked if they had ever had that house listed with their company. The answer was no.

He called the second one on his list. He got the same response.

He called the third and once again they had never listed the house but offered to go onto their computer and find the agent that had the house listed. The woman on the phone was able to give him the name and address of the company that sold the house.

Karst slapped his notebook on his leg saying, "Got it. Let's go."

Kent shook his head in disbelief.

Once inside the office, it was not difficult to find out who sold the house, and what service company was used to inspect the furnace before it sold.

Karst thanked the lady that helped him, and they were off to find someone they could talk to about the furnace in Isha's house.

The receptionist was not as organized as the woman at the real estate office. She dug through rumpled files and stacks of papers on her desk. She opened one file cabinet after another, confused as to where the file might have been.

Karst cringed just watching her. He held back the urge to start sorting and organizing the mess himself.

"Here it is," she said, proud of herself for finding it.

"Who was the serviceman who handled the inspection?" asked Karst.

She looked again.

"Oh, that was Rob. He's on a call this morning. No wait, that call was cancelled. Oh yeah, he's in the back today helping with some inventory," she remembered.

Karst and Kent walked past her and went to the back of the building. There were three men standing over some paperwork on a counter.

"Hey guys, Rob back here?" asked Karst.

"That'd be me," answered Rob.

"Glen Karst with the Denver Police," explained Karst as he shook hands with Rob. "I've got something here that you can help me with. Got a few minutes," asked Karst handing him the file that he took from the receptionist without giving her a chance to stop him.

"Uh, did I do something wrong?" asked Rob.

"No, I just need you to tell me, based on your notes here, what the condition of this furnace was the last time you inspected it."

Rob looked at the file.

"It says right here that furnace was put in new just before the house sold. It was in great shape," he said.

When Ashley ran into Stephanie's house she was sobbing uncontrollably. Stephanie looked up shocked.

"What's wrong?" she asked running to Ashley.

"Isha's dead. She and her husband died this morning. I'm scared. What's going on? Why are the kids dying just like our guys? Do you think Mark is doing it again? I'm terrified he'll hurt my kids. I don't think I can keep quiet much longer. I can't let him hurt my kids. I have to go to the police this time," cried Ashley.

"Oh my God, what happened to Isha?" questioned Stephanie.

"Her house exploded. They were killed instantly!"

Stephanie began to walk in circles around the room. She looked down at the carpet as she walked. She stopped and began to tap her toe, as she was deep in thought.

"Okay, listen. We don't know that Isha was murdered. It could've just been an accident. We are pretty quick to jump to conclusions, you know. And why would Mark kill his kids? He has nothing to gain by it, right? There just has to be some other explanation," insisted Stephanie.

"Detective Karst and Kent already stopped by this morning to give me the news. I feel so uncomfortable around Detective Karst. Sometimes I feel by the way he looks at me, he can read my mind. He gives me the creeps."

"Has Mark been notified?" asked Stephanie.

"Yes, they said they called him before they came over."

"What about Lexi? Has anyone called Lexi?" asked Stephanie.

"I'm not sure, I guess I thought Kent and Detective Karst would've stopped by her house before they came to see me."

"I'll call her and see if they paid her a visit this morning. Someone has to tell her," said Stephanie.

Ashley grabbed a phone book and looked up Lexi's phone number. Stephanie dialed the number. There was no answer at her home.

Susan walked in.

"Hi guys, are we still on for shopping this morning? There's this new restaurant I'd like to try for lunch if you two are game," announced Susan as she looked across the room at the two of them huddled near the phone.

"No, oh God no, I know that look. What happened?"

"Isha and her husband died this morning when their house exploded. Karst and Kent are investigating. They stopped by to talk to Ashley," explained Stephanie.

Susan studied Ashley. Her face was pale and she looked weak. Susan knew Ashley couldn't take much more of this.

"Was it an accident, or was she murdered?" asked Susan cutting right to the chase.

"We don't know," said Stephanie wringing her hands.

"Okay, you two get ready. We're out of here. We can sit here all day and worry or we can go somewhere else and worry. I'd just as soon not have Kent and Karst pop in on us here. Let's go shopping as planned just to get out of reach. We'll try to figure out what we are going to do next," suggested Susan.

"She's right, you know," said Stephanie to Ashley. "If Karst and Kent show up here, we would have a tough time pretending we know nothing."

Reluctantly, Ashley got up and followed the girls to Susan's car and they drove to the mall. They walked aimlessly around. No one shopped or even looked into the windows. They just walked. Occasionally one of them would try to come up with something to say to try to ease the suffering by suggesting Isha's death was really an accident.

"Oh shit!" exclaimed Stephanie. "Of all the days to just accidentally bump into Lexi."

"What? Where?" quizzed Ashley excitedly.

Stephanie moved over to the nearest window and pointed to the display. They all pretended to be interested in it.

Stephanie said, "Lexi and a friend are headed our way and I don't think we can avoid her."

Ashley added, "That means she doesn't know."

Susan suggested, "Let's take her aside and I'll walk with her until we find a quiet place to sit. I'll be the one to tell her."

They followed their plan. When Lexi saw them she smiled and waved. When she approached them they all gathered around Lexi and her friend.

Susan said, "Lexi, can you come with me a minute. I'd like to talk to you." She looked over her shoulder at her friend while Susan took her by the arm and escorted her away.

Ashley and Stephanie went up to Lexi's friend and explained what happened. She asked what she could do to help and they convinced her to just leave for now and they would take care of Lexi.

Susan found a couple of chairs away from the crowd and sat down with Lexi. She broke the news to her as gently as she could.

Lexi burst into tears. She sobbed so hard she nearly gagged. Slowly the others approached them.

Ashley squatted down in front of Lexi and hugged her. Lexi squeezed her so tightly she thought she would lose her balance from lack of air.

Susan and Stephanie each took one of Lexi's arms and helped her to her feet. She could barely walk. They asked her where she was parked and she explained she had come with her friend.

Ashley said, "We told your friend what happened and that we would take care of you. She left but said to call her if you need anything."

They walked her out to Susan's car and drove her home.

Once inside, Stephanie fixed her a cup of tea. They sat with her and answered questions to the best of their abilities. They really didn't have many of the facts themselves.

Stephanie was at a loss for words. She stood looking out the window, letting Ashley and Susan tend to Lexi. A car pulled up out front. She took a clearer look and realized it was Kent and Karst.

She looked at Susan and motioned for her to come to the window.

"Looks like we can't hide from them after all," Stephanie whispered.

Stephanie went to the door before they had a chance to ring the bell.

"Mom, what are you doing here?" asked Kent.

"We ran into Lexi at the mall, by looking at her, we knew no one had told her yet. Susan took her aside and explained what happened. She was in no condition to come home alone, so we came with her," explained Stephanie.

Karst walked over to Lexi, "Hello, I'm Detective Karst, I'm not sure if you remember me. We visited with you about your brother Trystan."

Lexi nodded her head.

"I'm so sorry about your loss. This has to be really tough on you. It's hard enough to lose one family member but no one should have to lose two so closely together. Are you up for a few questions?" asked Karst in a very gentle voice.

Lexi nodded again.

"Did Ashley tell you what happened?" asked Karst.

Lexi nodded again through her tears.

"We don't have a lot of information at the moment but it appears the furnace in the basement exploded causing the house to explode. One thing for sure is they died instantly in their sleep. She didn't suffer. I guess my only question to you would be did Isha tell you if anything was wrong with her furnace? I realize you probably don't know anything about it but I just wanted to stop by and be sure you were made aware of the accident."

Karst realized Lexi was too shaken up to speak and was about to leave when she blew her nose and cleared her throat. She managed the following words through her sobs, "They just had the furnace inspected."

Karst squatted back down next to her.

"How do you know that?"

"Isha was here last Tuesday and she was talking to her husband on the phone when he had to set the phone down to let the gasman into the basement to do a routine inspection of their furnace. That's all I know."

Karst patted her on the knee and said, "Thanks. Every little bit helps."

Karst stood up and turned to the Dolphins.

"Ladies," he said as he nodded his head good-bye.

Kent gave his mother a kiss on the cheek and followed Karst out the door.

Stephanie called Lexi's husband at work. He arrived shortly after Karst and Kent left.

The three women left so Lexi and her husband could be alone in their grief.

Susan drove Ashley back to her car at Stephanie's. They said their good-byes and Ashley drove home.

Before Karst and Kent even returned to the office, Karst had Kent call the gas company to see if they had sent a man out to inspect the furnace. They checked their records and told him no.

"Someone disguised as a gasman wormed his way into Isha's house and tampered with her furnace. I'm convinced this was no accident. The furnace was new and the coincidence of the mystery inspector is too strong," stated Karst.

Later that night at Ashley's, she was awakened by a sound coming from down the hall.

She crept out of bed and walked slowly down the hall. The door to Trystan's room was slightly ajar. She peeked in.

Standing over Trystan's desk was a man with his back to the door. Ashley gasped. She glanced over at the mirror across the room. It was Mark. In the mirror she saw him loading a gun.

Chapter 12

Instinctively, Ashley stepped back away from the door. She slid her back up against the wall. She stood motionless for a moment trying to decide if she should confront him or run to her room to call for help. But then again, who would she call? She'd have to call Stephanie or Amy. That could put their lives in danger. Was Mark there to kill her?

Her breathing quickened. Scenarios of death ran through her mind. How would my children cope without me? What should I do? What should I do? Those were her thoughts racing at that moment.

Finally it came to her. She would set off her alarm system. When the police arrived she would just tell them her husband came home unexpectedly and it was all a mistake. Mark would have to stash the gun. If she showed up dead later the police would know Mark was in the house with her. He was smart enough to figure out the same thing. She knew she could save her own life by letting the police know he was there. She slipped down the hall to trigger the alarm.

She locked herself in her room, then pressed the panic button she had installed in her bedroom. She took the phone off of the hook so the police could not call to check if everything was okay, and she waited. It wasn't long at all and there were two police cars in her driveway and a knock at her door. She ran down the stairs to let them in.

Mark appeared at the top of the stairs wondering what was going on and soon joined Ashley.

"Mrs. Wilson your silent alarm system went off and we are here to be sure everything is okay," said the officer.

"I'm not sure why it went off," lied Ashley.

She turned to look at Mark as he approached her.

"Mark, when did you get home? I wasn't expecting you."

Before Mark could answer Ashley turned back to the officer and explained, " I'm sorry. This is my husband. He must've accidentally set off the alarm when he came home. Everything is okay. Sorry to have you come out in the middle of the night."

"No problem, Mrs. Wilson, we're just doing our job. Good night," he said and he left.

Ashley locked the door behind them. She leaned her back up against the wall facing Mark.

"Would you like to tell me what you are doing here?" she demanded.

"Surely you knew I'd be here as quickly as possible. You know what happened to Isha don't you?"

"Of course I know. What I want to know is how could you kill your own kids?" she asked.

Mark's eyes glared at her. He was furious. His face became red. He almost hit her but pulled his punch. Instead he punched the wall next to her. His blow to the wall was hard enough he split his knuckles open; blood began to drip onto the floor.

"Feel better?" asked Ashley sarcastically.

She went to the bathroom for first aid supplies.

When she returned, Mark had gone into the kitchen to run cool water over his wounded hand.

Ashley went to him. She dried his hand, applied an ointment, and then bandaged it. Even though she was furious with him the gentle side of her still forced her to care for his wound.

"I saw you upstairs with a gun. What are you planning to do with it?"

Mark hesitated for a moment, surprised that Ashley knew about the gun.

"I plan to carry it with me to protect myself," he answered.

"Why did you bring it here?" she asked.

"I didn't bring it here, it was here already. I had it hidden downstairs in my shop. I had the bullets hidden in Trystan's room. After I went to the basement for the gun I went upstairs to load it. Someone is killing my kids and I may be next."

Ashley studied his face for a long while.

She believed he didn't kill Trystan.

"No one knows for sure about Isha's death. Maybe it really was an accident," stated Ashley.

"Isha's death was no accident. I got another CD delivered to me. It was Stephanie's voice from the party describing Richard's death by explosion. I thought I would be killed in an explosion until I got the phone call from Kent telling me about Isha. Don't you see, whoever it is wants to punish me. Whoever it is wants me to sit back and watch my family be murdered one by one."

"And I'm supposed to feel sorry for you?" asked Ashley. "I feel sorry for your kids. They were innocent victims paying the price for what you did to all of us. But then again, our husbands were innocent victims of your plan to kill Theresa. I have no sympathy for you."

Mark hung his head feeling defeated.

"Ashley, I'm sorry. Theresa made me crazy. You have no idea what it was like being married to her. I couldn't take it any more. When the idea came to me, I just took it and ran with it. I didn't care about anyone or anything other than removing Theresa from my life. I couldn't let her continue to raise our kids. I wanted to spare them from her. I was afraid of the emotional damage they would suffer with her as their mother. It wasn't until now that I truly understand the pain I put all of you through."

"Once it was over I spent the next years worrying someone would find out. Everyone thought it was Theresa, and with her dead, I felt I was safe. I had to be aware of everything you girls were doing. I needed to know that you were keeping it a secret. That's the only reason I made those recordings. Once Melissa started snooping around, I was sure she had learned about my recordings. I had to stop her. She was so much like Theresa. She really didn't like me. Letting her live might have caused me to be caught. I just couldn't let that happen."

Ashley did not want to forgive him or even try to understand what drove him to the murders, but a part of her felt sorry for him. Deep down she could actually understand the point he was trying to make. The desperate means a parent will take to protect his children.

Ashley went to the cabinet and took down two cups. She filled the teapot with water. She scooped instant coffee into their cups and waited for the water to heat.

"So now what? If it's not you and it's not me who's sending you the recordings?"

"I'm not sure. In the beginning I thought the first tape was given to me after Trystan's death as a bad sick joke. The second CD came to me before Isha died," said Mark.

221

"Did it? I mean could someone have seen the explosion or knew about it and sent the CD immediately to you?" asked Ashley.

"Not likely. Think about it, Ashley. There wouldn't have been enough time. I'm sure the CD was on its way to New York before Isha's house exploded," Mark pointed out.

"Yeah, I suppose you're right," agreed Ashley.

The teapot began to whistle. Mark got up to get it and poured the hot water over the instant coffee. Talking to Ashley comforted him. It's the first time in years they could talk to each other without fighting.

"Do you have any idea who it could be?" asked Ashley.

"I think I do but I don't think you are going to agree with me," replied Mark.

"Who?" Ashley demanded.

"Well, we know that all of the Dolphins are aware of the tape from the party. I'm just not sure how they would have gotten a copy. I think it's Stephanie. She mysteriously moved to Denver out of the blue, she definitely hates me, she had access to my kids, she knew your address in New York where I live, and I killed her husband. If I had to choose, I'd say it was her."

"Stephanie? I'm not sure I'd choose Stephanie, but then again it could be any of the girls if you want to go accusing them. Take Amy for example. She hates you and she lives here. She knows about the tapes, you killed her husband."

"Or how about Susan? She moved to Denver, she hates you, you killed her husband, and her daughter Megan never coped with his death and the new baby sister. She walked out of Susan's life and it devastated her," reminded Ashley.

"You're right. It could be any one of them," agreed Mark.

"One more thing you should know," confessed Ashley. "I copied the tapes before I returned them to your file cabinet. Then I gave copies to all of the girls so if anything happened to any one of us the others had a copy to go to the police with. But I still don't think any one of them is guilty," insisted Ashley.

They both sat back and sipped their coffee. It has to be someone and Mark is right. It must be one of the girls, who else could it be? Ashley thought.

Mark broke the silence, "It's getting late, and we should get some sleep. I need to be with Lexi tomorrow."

They left the kitchen and went to their separate bedrooms to try to sleep.

Karst was pacing around his office. Kent sat in a chair watching him.

"Damn, there has to be some way to connect the dots on all these mysterious deaths," said Karst referring to the deaths surrounding Ashley.

"Well let's get to work then," suggested Kent.

"Okay, smart guy, what do you suggest," remarked Karst a little irritated.

"Why don't we just work our way backwards in time?" suggested Kent.

"You mean first Isha's death then Trystan's?" asked Karst.

"Yeah, but let's throw Melissa's death in there and keep going backwards," answered Kent.

"I'll try anything at this point. Let's do it," agreed Karst.

He set Isha's file on his desk then to the left of it he placed Trystan's file. Following that he put Melissa's file next to Trystan's.

They looked at the files almost expecting an answer to jump out at them.

Karst took his key out and unlocked the drawer. He thumbed through the files.

"What are you looking for?" asked Kent.

"Remember I told you death seems to linger around Mrs. Wilson? Let's take a look at the deaths that I investigated when she was interviewed," commented Karst.

He couldn't remember the names of the victims after so many years and so many files. He had hoped the names would remind him, but they didn't and many more had been added to the drawer over the past years.

Upset for not remembering he grabbed half of the files for himself and gave the other half to Kent.

"See if you can find the case of the man that died at the Adams Mark hotel from anaphylactic shock," instructed Karst.

Kent had barely begun his search when Karst burst out, "Saunders! The guy's name was Saunders. Check your stack."

Karst was relieved that his memory had not failed him completely; it just needed a little jolt.

Kent checked his stack and there it was, Brian Saunders. He put the other files back in the drawer.

Karst snatched the file from the desk and began skimming it. All of the facts were coming back to him now. He read his notes from his interview with Ashley. Nothing out of the ordinary appeared.

"Oh yeah, this guy was from back east, not here. Says here his wife's name was Susan. Wait a minute. It says here that the night her husband was murdered, or I mean, died, Susan was staying the night with the Wilson's. That puts Mark in the running," reported Karst.

"Susan?" said Kent. "My mom's friend is Susan. She used to live back east until she recently moved here. Let me see that file. It just gives her name and address and the details of her interview. Says here she was at Ashley's house when you did your final interview."

"That's right, remember, I told you I'd been there before for two deaths," reminded Karst.

"Who was the other death?" asked Kent.

"It was Ashley's husband," replied Karst.

225

Kent looked in the drawer, but there was no file on Ashley's husband.

"I can't find a file for him here," said Kent.

"Well his name would be Moore the same name Ashley uses for her books," Karst explained.

Kent looked again. "Still not here," he said.

"I'm a little shaky on that one. There must not have been much to it to arouse any suspicion. I obviously didn't keep the file. Why don't you see if you can run it down while I look through these," suggested Karst.

Kent returned with the file. Karst took it from him.

"I didn't find anything new in the other files. Seems Ashley's husband Michael died of an asthma attack. Nothing unusual there," sighed Karst disappointed.

"There just has to be something we're missing. Wait, Mark and Ashley got married. What happened to the original Mrs. Wilson?" questioned Karst.

"My mom said she was a real witch. Her name was Theresa. She and Mark were dating in high school when they broke up Ashley and Mark started dating. Theresa showed up pregnant by Mark, so Mark dumped Ashley and married Theresa," reported Kent.

"Wait, you said her name was Theresa?" asked Karst. He grabbed the file on Mr. Saunders again and read through the interviews. "Here, right here, Theresa Wilson was interviewed at the Adams Mark along with Ashley and Susan."

226

"Yeah, that would be her. They were all school chums back in high school. My mom said they called themselves the Dolphins because of some swim team they were on," said Kent.

"Okay, let's get this straight. Your mom, Stephanie, was a friend to Ashley and Susan and Theresa. Mark was married to Theresa and now Ashley. Susan's husband died. Ashley's husband died. Where's Theresa?" asked Karst.

"She's dead too," answered Kent.

"So we have four women that were friends. Two of their husbands and one of the women are now dead," said Karst as he wrote all of this on his board on the wall.

"My dad also died," commented Kent. "My mom is remarried."

"Now we have four married couples and four dead spouses. That's sharing a little too closely. What are the dates on these deaths?" asked Karst.

"My dad died before I was born, actually, before I was conceived," started Kent.

Karst looked up at him. "Now do tell, how did that happen?"

"Frozen embryos. That's where my brother and I came from," explained Kent.

"Was your dad ill, and they planned ahead?" asked Karst.

"No," said Kent, "He died in an explosion. Mom was so upset; she wanted to have dad's kids since she

227

could no longer have him. She arranged to have me, then, Tom to make up for not having my dad."

"Get on the computer and find out what you can about Theresa Wilson's death and the date," Karst ordered.

Karst erased his board and started again. He listed the name of the women down one side. He made columns to follow the names: husband's name, cause of death and date of death.

Kent returned with the information.

"Theresa was killed by an accident at a remote control plane park. It seems she lost control of her plane and it flew right into her head. She died instantly," reported Kent.

"Boy, that's one weird way to go. Okay, let's have the date," said Karst with his arm raised to fill in his chart.

"Her accident was on August 5th, 2000," answered Kent.

Karst stood back and looked at his chart. "We have a death in August, one in July, and one in June all in the year 2000," he remarked. "Just out of curiosity, when did your dad die?"

"It was on the 4th of July. Let's see, I was born in 2001. My dad died the 4th of July of 2000," replied Kent.

"Why am I not surprised?" asked Karst as he added Kent's dad to his chart. "I'm telling you, Kent, this is not normal."

"What does it mean?" asked Kent.

"I'm not sure, but this makes me feel uncomfortable," admitted Karst. "So you say your mother and these women belonged to a gang called the Dolphins?"

Kent laughed. "I'd hardly call it a gang. They were pretty much all goody two shoes. They were just a bunch of rich kids that stuck together like glue according to my mom. She used to show us pictures of them together in her yearbook before we'd come to visit Ashley for Christmas."

"Why would you come to visit Ashley for Christmas?" quizzed Karst.

"Oh about every five years they wanted to get together so they would drag all of us kids there and my mom and her friends would reminisce while we were properly fed, spoiled and entertained. One year Ashley even hired a Santa to come to the house," remembered Kent.

"How touching," teased Karst. "Is there any way you could get your hands on that yearbook without your mom knowing about it?" asked Karst.

"I'm sure we could just go to the school library and look up a copy. They went to school here in Denver," suggested Kent.

"Let's go," said Karst.

Once they arrived at the school library, the search was on for the yearbook. They knew within two years when the girls had graduated. It didn't take long before they found the book from their graduating class. They grabbed the three books from the previous years and sat at a table to look through them.

From their freshman year through their senior year they were always together in the photos. They joined all of the same clubs, went out for the same sports and worked on the same committees.

The one fact they were surprised, but pleased to find, was there were two more Dolphins missing from Karst's chart on the wall.

"I wonder what the story is with these two?" asked Karst.

"I can tell you this one here, Amy. She's a judge now. She used to come to the Christmas parties. She didn't have any kids. I'm not sure if she was ever married," explained Kent.

"Judge Issacson...hmm...doesn't ring a bell. Is she from Denver?" asked Karst.

"Yeah, my mom and Ashley and Susan run around with her on girl's night out."

"Hey, do me a favor and call your mom and ask her what Amy's name is," pleaded Karst.

"Now?" asked Kent.

"Yes, right now. Just call her and ask her. Make up some excuse why you want to know."

"Okay, here goes," remarked Kent as he dialed the phone.

Stephanie answered.

"Hey mom, I'm at the courthouse and I'll be sitting in on a trial with a woman judge. What's Amy's last name? I thought it might be her," lied Kent.

"Roth, her name is Roth. You'll have to let me know how she performs, I've heard she's tough," laughed Stephanie.

"Nope, sorry, that's not the same name. I'll call ya later. Bye." Kent hung up.

"You're getting pretty good at this stuff," teased Karst. "What'd you find out?"

"My mom said her name is Roth. I guess that means she was married once," answered Kent.

"Whoa, Judge Roth. I'm sure she wouldn't want her name connected to all of this. Now we need to find out what happened to Mr. Roth. Did they divorce, or is he dead as well?"

"We forgot this one. Brittany. I vaguely remember my mom mentioning a Brittany but I sure couldn't tell you anything about her. She never came to any of the Christmas parties," stated Kent.

"Well, lad," whispered Karst, slapping Kent on the back. "I think you need to take your mother out to dinner again. We need some more information."

"Great! Mom always picks up the tab, and she likes to eat at places I can't afford on my salary," laughed Kent.

Kent and Karst left the library to go back to the office. On the way, Kent called his mother to make plans for dinner that night.

"Hi mom, it's me again. Say, I was wondering if your favorite son can take you to dinner tonight?" teased Kent.

"Wow, does that mean Tom's in town?" joked Stephanie.

"Ha, ha, ha. A guy wants to take his mom out on the town and she insults him," whined Kent.

"I'd love to, dear, but the girls and I are going out to eat tonight. Can we make it for tomorrow night instead?" pleaded Stephanie.

"Sure, not a problem, I handle rejection pretty well," groaned Kent.

Feeling guilty, Stephanie suggested, "Why don't you join us tonight? The girls would love to see you. I won't take no for an answer. I'll even buy your dinner."

"How could any guy in his right mind refuse a free dinner with four gorgeous chicks?" teased Kent. "Just tell me where and when, or would you like me to pick you up?"

"Sure, pick me up at seven," replied Stephanie.

Kent agreed, "Seven it is. See ya tonight. Bye."

Karst turned to Kent, "Sounds good, you're having dinner with your mom, right?"

"Yep and the rest of the Dolphins as well. A few glasses of wine and I'll start asking them questions about

232

their youth. I think we'll learn a lot from tonight's dinner party."

Karst drove back to his office. He and Kent added the two new names to the chart on the wall.

"Tomorrow when you come in you'd better be able to fill in the blanks for me. I'm counting on you," said Karst.

"Oh ye of little faith," laughed Kent. "I'll charm the pants off those ladies. You should see me in action."

"Yeah, well, if you're such a charmer why isn't there a woman in your life, Mr. Bachelor?" joked Karst.

"Oh man, speaking of a woman in your life, Debbie has company coming for dinner in about ten minutes. She's gonna shoot me. I promised this time I wouldn't be late," yelled Karst as he ran out the door.

Lexi clung to Mark for support while they made arrangements for Isha's burial. Isha's husband's family wanted to bury Isha with their son, but Mark wanted to bury her with Trystan. Eventually, the other family gave in. They agreed to have joint services with separate plots.

Mark was fearful for Lexi's life. He wanted to tell her to be careful, but once again he found himself in the same situation the Dolphins were in years ago; warning someone meant including them in the secret. Exposing the secret meant being found out and prosecuted for the murders. He decided instead not to leave her side. He kept his gun with him at all times. He was going to protect her from the maniac that was killing his kids.

233

Making arrangements for the funeral went quickly. It hadn't been that long since the arrangements were made for Trystan.

Mark decided to retire from his business and move permanently back to Denver so he could watch Lexi more closely. He hadn't been working much this last year, anyway.

Lexi became very depressed. Before the accident, she and her husband had begun construction on a new house. They postponed all plans. Mark tried to help Lexi cope. He suggested she focus on the new house project again. He told her he would help her make decisions about designs and decorating.

Lexi was reluctant to get started again, but Mark insisted. Her husband was pleased Mark was there to help her through this while he was at work.

Their routine began. Lexi's husband would leave for work. Mark would stop by after breakfast and pick her up. They would drive out into the country where the house was to be built. After parking the car, they would walk down the path to the construction site. The weather was warm; they would sit on a blanket and make plans. Day in and day out, the routine was the same.

Up until that point, all that had begun on the new home was the foundation. The basement was poured; no further work was done on the main portion of the house. With Mark's urging, Lexi and her husband made arrangements for the contractors to begin work again soon.

Mark was happy to feel needed. He still carried his gun with him everywhere without Lexi's knowledge. There were no more tapes and no more accidents. He was wondering what would happen next.

One day while following their routine, Mark and Lexi were walking around the foundation of the house planning how the landscaping would look when all was finished. Mark had the urge to relieve himself and went off into the trees, leaving Lexi alone.

When he returned he didn't see her. He called her name but there was no answer. He continued to walk around the grounds looking for her. He was confused. He walked to the foundation and looked down into the basement. There on the concrete floor of the basement lay Lexi's limp body in a pool of her blood. Lexi's black hair covered her face.

Mark could tell she was unconscious but before he climbed down to check on her he called 911 and gave them directions. He closed his cell phone and searched for a ladder or rope or anything he could use to lower himself down to where Lexi lay.

He found cargo straps from the trailer that hauled the lumber to the site in a heap near the trees. He went to gather them up to lower himself down. When he bent down to pick up the straps something hard came down and hit him on the head. He was dazed. He turned and saw a person dressed in black with a stocking cap over the face. They struggled. Mark could barely stand on his feet. His vision was blurred. Mark went for his gun and the masked person knocked it out of his hand. The struggle continued until the two of them were near the foundation once again. Mark reached to put his hands around the throat of his assailant. The masked person came up between Mark's arms breaking the hold. Mark lost his footing and fell backwards into the basement. Before the assailant could climb down to confirm they were both dead the sound of sirens approaching could be heard.

Chapter 13

Kent and his mother arrived at the restaurant right on time. They took a table for five and waited. Susan and Ashley arrived a few minutes later.

"Kent, what a pleasant surprise. What's the occasion?" asked Susan.

"My loving son here wanted to take his mother out to dinner tonight. I told him I had plans with you girls and invited him to join us. He graciously accepted. Of course, I had to bribe him with my offer to pay," teased Stephanie.

The others laughed and Kent took the abuse.

"Where's Amy?" asked Ashley. "She's usually the first one here, complaining all the rest of us are late."

"I haven't seen her yet," replied Stephanie.

"There she is, over there," pointed Susan as she waved her hand in the air to get Amy's attention.

Amy joined them.

"What happened to your hand?" asked Ashley.

Amy's hand and wrist were bandaged.

"Oh nothing, I just slipped in the bathroom on wet tiles and put my hands out to break my fall. I sprained my wrist. It'll be fine," explained Amy.

"When did it happen?" asked Stephanie.

"Just today," answered Amy, adjusting the bandage.

"Didn't you work today?" asked Susan.

"Okay, if you must know, I've lightened my schedule and I'm thinking about retiring," announced Amy.

"What?" responded the other three women simultaneously.

"I can't believe my ears. Judge Amy Roth, the ultimate career woman is considering retiring," teased Ashley.

"What brought this on?" asked Stephanie.

"I just think it's time. I mean, William and I want to spend more time together," admitted Amy.

"Who's William?" asked Kent.

"He's the elusive boyfriend of Amy's. She's never even introduced him to us, and now he's convinced her to quit her job. Things must be serious," joked Stephanie.

"You should talk. How many times have you brought Alex around us?" reminded Amy.

"Why would I want Alex to know how crazy my friends truly are?" laughed Stephanie.

"Really why don't we see more of Alex?" asked Susan.

"Oh, I don't know. When he's home and not traveling we like to spend quiet time together. He's really not much into group things. He kind of likes to keep me to himself. He's a little overprotective, but I love it. Besides, with this group, he'd always be the only man," Stephanie pointed out.

"And what does that make me?" asked Kent.

The others laughed.

"Okay, okay, if Amy invites William to a dinner, I'll bring Kent and Alex. Then none of them would have to feel awkward," said Stephanie.

The waiter came to take their orders. As the evening progressed, the wine flowed, just as Kent had hoped. The girls were getting a little silly, and the conversation was turning more personal.

"So Amy, do you see you and this William guy getting married someday?" asked Kent.

"Maybe," answered Amy.

"You've been single your whole life. What do you think adjusting to married life would be like?" questioned Kent.

"Oh Amy's been married before," commented Ashley.

"I'm sorry, I didn't know," lied Kent. "What happened?"

Amy, who always drinks more than the others, was feeling pretty high at that moment.

"Someone shot the son of a bitch," she blurted out.

239

Kent was surprised. The others looked around to see if any of the other customers heard her as they tried to quiet her down.

Susan began, "Amy was married to a man named Jonathon. He wasn't a very good husband. He played around with all of his female clients. He was a divorce attorney. Anyway, he played around with the wrong woman, and someone shot him and the woman."

"When did that happen?" quizzed Kent.

"June 8th, 2000, the happiest day of my life," announced Amy. "I'll never forget it." She raised her glass of wine in a toast to Jonathon's death.

Kent was excited that she told him. He was anxious to see Karst's reaction the next morning that yet another husband had died that same summer.

The girls talked and drank the rest of the evening away. Kent didn't drink but encouraged them to so he could gather more information.

"Were all four of you part of the Dolphin group?" asked Kent.

"Actually, there were six of us in all," responded Susan.

"Really, who were the others?" asked Kent.

"Well there was Brittany Armstrong and Theresa Davidson," reported Ashley.

"I know Theresa died, but what ever happened to Brittany?" asked Kent

"Poor Brittany. After her husband died, she submerged herself in her kids, and I guess you could say, dropped out of our group. She felt being around us was too strong a reminder of her past and she wanted to move forward and not look back," explained Susan. "Everyone has a different way of dealing with his or her grief."

"I thought you were retired, Doc," teased Amy.

"I am, Kent wanted to know what happened to Brittany and I felt he needed an explanation as to why she was no longer part of our little group here," explained Susan defensively.

"How did Brittany's husband die?" asked Kent.

Suddenly, the girls began to sober up. They realized that speaking to Kent was nearly the same as speaking directly to Detective Karst.

Stephanie answered Kent, "He had a construction accident. He fell to his death. But that was a long time ago. Dessert, anyone?"

Stephanie was hoping to change the subject. She knew her son was very clever and she didn't want him to begin putting pieces of the puzzle together.

Kent did not want to disappoint Karst. He had to get the last bit of information.

"How long ago did he die?" quizzed Kent trying to get them back on the subject.

"Oh that was before you were born," answered Stephanie.

"That's right," started Amy drunkenly. "He was the first one to die. That was the spring of 2000. Yep, Robert Lane was the first of them all."

"Amy, come with me to ladies room," suggested Ashley as she pulled Amy up from her chair.

Ashley felt Amy needed to move around and sober up before she told Kent something they would all regret.

Stephanie took the opportunity while Amy was away from the table to suggest she and Kent leave.

"Alex is home waiting and I'm sure Kent has an early morning. I think we'll take off now," announced Stephanie.

Kent slid his chair back and stood to help his mother with her chair. He kissed Susan on the cheek as he bid her goodnight. Ashley and Amy didn't return to the table until Kent and Stephanie had already gone.

The next morning, Kent arrived at the office before Karst. He brought coffee and donuts. He was pleased with himself. He went to the chart on Karst's wall and filled in the blanks.

Karst stepped into his office. He noticed the donuts and grabbed one as he sat down at his desk. His eyes caught sight of his chart. He set his donut down and walked over to the wall.

"So Brittany had a husband die from a construction accident in the same year as the rest of the deaths. His eyes continued down the chart. Judge Roth's

242

old man was shot and killed during a love affair the same year. How interesting," Karst remarked.

He stood there for a long time reading everything on the chart over and over. He began erasing and changing the order of the names. He put them in date order of the deaths.

"In just four months all of the deaths happened. All appear to be accidents except for Judge Roth's hmm..." whispered Karst.

Kent looked at him.

Karst stopped for a moment. He wondered if it was a good idea to continue working with Kent on this, since his father was one of the victims if these were not accidental deaths.

"Are you thinking the accidents are connected in some way?" quizzed Kent. "Even my dad's?"

"I'm not saying they are, and I'm not saying they're not. A good detective looks at facts from every angle," stated Karst.

Karst sent Kent on an errand. He called Thompson into the room.

"Hey, take a look at this mess. Here we have two recent deaths of a brother and a sister. One was a definite murder the other a possibility. Now, when you look at the father, he was connected to a group of couples, that over twenty years ago, lost six spouses out of six marriages. I think I'm on to something big here, but I don't know what yet. The kicker is the Nolan kid is my lead to find out information. His mother is one of the original six couples. The bad thing is he may be investigating the death of his own father and we may be talking murder here. I think I need to pull him from the case, but damn I need him. What would you do in my situation?" questioned Karst.

"Well, you know I'm not fond of you babysitting this guy, but I agree you really need him. I'd say keep him on as long as you can and don't give him all of your details. When and if things begin to look like his old man's death was not an accident, I'd send him packing. You're here to do a job, so don't get so attached to this kid that he interferes with your investigation," said Thompson.

"Thanks," replied Karst. "That's what I'll do. I was leaning along the same path anyway, but needed some input to be sure my emotions weren't getting in the way."

Although Thompson and Karst had a history of butting heads on many occasions, when it came to actually working on a case, they were good together. Karst thought maybe he should bring Thompson in on this without informing Kent of his plan to do so.

Ashley was having her morning cup of coffee when she realized there was no sign of Mark being up yet. He was always up before her. He usually had the coffee going for her when she woke. In the past he never drank coffee, couldn't stand the taste, but when he needed to stay awake all hours working on some music project, he learned to drink it. Now he was addicted, just like everyone else that has to have that morning cup.

She sat at her kitchen table reading the paper and sipping her coffee. Finally, she couldn't stand wondering whether or not Mark was there. She went up to his room. The bed was made and there was no sign of him. Even if he had left early that morning, he still would have started the coffee.

As the morning passed she wondered even more about his whereabouts. She remembered his fear that someone was planning to kill him. She called Susan.

"Hi Susan, it's me, Ash. I just needed to talk about Mark. He didn't come home last night."

"I'd think you'd be grateful," replied Susan.

"Normally I would, but he confided in me he thought someone was out to kill him and now that he didn't come home, it has me wondering," admitted Ashley.

"Did you try his cell phone?" asked Susan.

"Yeah, it wasn't on," answered Ashley.

"Didn't you say he spends his days with Lexi?" questioned Susan.

"I already called her. There was no answer," replied Ashley.

Susan said, "There you have it. They must've had an early day planned. Maybe he spent the night with her and her husband. He doesn't have to check in with you now, does he?"

"Of course not," responded Ashley feeling foolish for caring. "He can come and go as he pleases. I just thought it was a little odd."

The house seemed extremely quiet that morning. Ashley no longer kept Carol on as her assistant. She didn't want her around Mark. Ashley was unsure just how unstable Mark was. She didn't want to take any chances that there would be a repeat to Melissa's murder.

She went to her study to write. The doorbell rang. She ran to answer it. A messenger delivered a package for Mark. She signed for it. She tipped the delivery boy and tossed the package on the end table near the sofa. She sat on the sofa staring at the package. She remembered Mark telling her about the CDs that he had received surrounding the deaths of his kids. Could this be another?

She went back to her study to continue writing. She sat looking at a blank computer screen. Nothing came to her. She realized her mind was on the package. Mark didn't come home and then a package arrived. Was there a connection?

She heard Stephanie call from the other room, "Ash, are you home?"

All of the girls had keys to each other's houses. They felt safer that way. Ashley walked into the living room to join Stephanie.

"Hi, what are you doing here?" asked Ashley.

"Oh nothing, Alex left to play golf this morning, and I had no plans for the day so, I thought I'd bug you for awhile. How'd things go with Amy after we left last night?" quizzed Stephanie.

246

"We didn't stay much longer. Did anything that was said last night cause any suspicion with Kent?" asked Ashley.

"If it did, he didn't say anything to me. Actually, I think he thinks anything connected to his mother has to be pretty boring," admitted Stephanie.

"Mark didn't come home last night," Ashley blurted out of nowhere. "I'm not sure what happened to him."

"What makes you think anything happened to him?" asked Stephanie.

"He thinks someone is trying to kill him, and all of his kids. I have to admit I might agree with him considering the way things have been happening around here. This package was delivered here for him this morning and I'm tempted to open it," confided Ashley.

"So open it. What's the big deal? Just tell him you thought it was for you."

"Do you really think I should?" asked Ashley, hoping for a little more encouragement.

"Oh, hell," remarked Stephanie. "I'll do it if you don't have the nerve to. What's he gonna do, shoot us?"

"That's not funny," whined Ashley.

Stephanie grabbed the package and tore the strip that opened it. Inside was a CD.

"It's probably from one of his clients," explained Stephanie as she walked across the room to put it in the CD player and listen to it.

Ashley watched her from across the room. She kept one eye peeled for the door in case Mark did walk in.

The voice from the speakers filled the room. It was Brittany and her soft voice quivering as she planned Robert's death at his cabin construction site. Stephanie turned it off quickly. She put it back in the package and set the package back on the end table.

She looked up at Ashley.

Ashley was white.

"I don't get it. What's it mean?" quizzed Stephanie.

"Mark says when Trystan died, someone sent him a copy of the tape with Theresa's voice talking about the plane accident. Trystan died in a plane accident. Later, when Isha died, Mark received a recording of your voice talking about Richard's death by explosion. Isha died in an explosion. Now this. It must mean someone will die, or has died, by a construction accident."

"I'll bet Mark is sending these recordings to himself to throw us off. I'll bet he's responsible for the deaths of his own kids to cover his own butt. He knows we know and he's trying to convince us he's the victim now," stated Stephanie.

"I don't know. I think I believe him. But your theory makes the most sense. No one knows about the taped party except for Mark and the rest of us," commented Ashley.

"Actually, I have a confession to make. I told Alex," announced Stephanie.

248

"You did what?" exploded Ashley. "How could you? We all promised each other that secret would stay between us until the day we died. We agreed not to tell anyone."

"I know, and I'm sorry. I just couldn't marry him and hide that from him. I needed him to know. I needed him to be safe and aware that Mark was capable of anything. I let him listen to the copy you gave me," admitted Stephanie.

"Great, that's just great. I wonder who he's told?" asked Ashley.

"He's never mentioned it again since the day he heard it. He wanted to go to the police then, and I convinced him he would cause damage to too many people's lives and what was done was done. Now you know why you never see him. He doesn't want to take the chance of being in the same room with Mark. He hates him, and he's never even met him. He's a gentle man, but he does have a temper. I really think our secret is safe with him."

"I think we need to call the others and tell them about Mark missing, the CD that came today and the fact you included Alex in on our little secret. I don't think they are going to be too happy. I'll see if I can reach Susan and Amy," said Ashley thoroughly disgusted with Stephanie.

Susan was still home when Ashley called her and asked her to come over. Amy was not. She reached Amy on her cell phone.

"Are you working today?" asked Ashley.

"No, why?" asked Amy.

"I need you to come by right away if you can."

Amy asked, "Why, what's up?"

"I'll tell you when you get here," said Ashley as she hung up the phone before Amy could get another question in.

Kent returned to the office. Karst was gone to follow up on an accident report that came across his desk. He left a note for Kent with a list of things for him to work on. He wanted to begin to wean Kent from the case.

Karst arrived at the hospital to talk to the two people brought in late yesterday afternoon; one was Mark, the other was Lexi. They were both still alive. Lexi was still unconscious, but Mark had regained consciousness just before Karst had arrived. The doctors were examining him and asking him questions when Karst walked into his room.

"Good morning Mr. Wilson," started Karst. "Are you feeling well enough to answer a few questions?"

At the same time Karst shot a glance at one of the doctors to be sure it was okay for him to ask Mark questions. The doctor nodded his head in approval.

"I have to know how my daughter Lexi is first," demanded Mark.

The doctor stepped forward again.

"Mr. Wilson, she still hasn't regained consciousness but her vitals are strong. We're hoping for the best," he said.

"What happened to you?" asked Karst.

"My memory's a little shaky but I was with my daughter, we were walking around the area where she is building her new home. She fell into the basement. I called 911. The next thing I remember was waking up here. I must've fallen in trying to climb down to help her," lied Mark.

"Mr. Wilson, I have to know, was any one else there?" asked Karst.

"No sir, we were alone," replied Mark.

"Why so many accidents involving your family lately? Do you think someone is trying to hurt you or your kids?"

"I don't know. I can't think of anyone. I don't know why anyone would want to hurt me or my kids," Mark lied once more.

"Okay, you just rest. That's all for now," stated Karst.

Karst stepped out into the hall. He tipped his head back. He knew he was onto something. He felt Mark was hiding something. He felt Ashley was hiding something. He knew he had to approach this carefully. He rubbed his chin between his fingers while he planned his next move. He decided to go over to Ashley's and see what he could learn from her.

Amy and Susan joined Ashley and Stephanie.

"We're here, what's the big mystery?" asked Amy.

251

"You're not still worried about Mark not coming home last night, are you?" asked Susan.

"Don't even tell me you called us here because that jerk husband of yours stayed out all night and you're concerned about him," scolded Amy.

"Just chill," said Stephanie.

Ashley began, "You're right, Mark didn't come home last night. Then later this morning he received a package by messenger. Stephanie and I opened it and there was a CD in it with Brittany's voice talking about Robert's death. It was from the party."

"Brittany sent Mark a CD?" questioned Amy.

"No, that's not what happened. Someone sent it to Mark, but I doubt if it was Brittany. I never gave her a copy of it. Anyway, let me go on," insisted Ashley. "Mark received a portion of the tape when each of his kids died. Then this morning another portion arrived and Mark didn't come home last night. Stephanie thinks he's sending them to himself to cover his trail. She also thinks he's killing his own kids to protect himself by making us think he's the victim. The other thing I have to tell you is going to make you mad, but please contain yourselves," begged Ashley.

"I'll tell them. After all, I'm the one that broke our promise," started Stephanie. "I told Alex about the murders and the slumber party and the tapes and that Mark was responsible."

"You've got to be kidding. Tell me you're kidding," pleaded Amy. "Have you any idea what you've done to us?"

"I know, I know, but I explained to Alex that he needed to keep our secret. I told him not to ruin your lives for something that happened in the past. He wanted to go to the police, but I talked him out of it. I told him before we were even married. He's kept our secret so far and I trust he always will," said Stephanie.

"I'm sure glad Friday is my last day. I always feared being removed from the seat if this scandal ever got out. Now I know I can be a retired judge in jail. Not that I'd last very long with all the losers I've put behind bars as roommates," groaned Amy.

"Okay guys, now that you're here, we need to figure out what's going on. Who's sending the recordings and who's hurting Mark's kids and how do we stop whoever it is without hurting ourselves?" questioned Ashley.

"I, for one, still think Mark's doing it all," said Stephanie.

"To be honest with you Ash, if it's not Mark, I'd prefer we just sit back and let whoever it is finish him off. I feel sorry for his kids, but there's nothing we can do to protect Lexi. It would be better for her if Mark were dead. Then maybe whoever it is will stop. Can't punish a dead man," remarked Amy.

"Susan? Any ideas?" asked Ashley.

"Nope, I'm at a loss for words. If it's not Mark, we're back to square one. It has to be one of us. We've been through this before. I need time to think this through," responded Susan.

"There's always Stephanie's new man, Alex. He knows, so he has to be figured into the equation with us. The only other person is Theresa and I know if she could find a way to come back from the dead and seek revenge I'm sure she would've done so years ago," stated Amy.

The doorbell rang. Ashley went to answer.

Detective Karst said, "Hello Mrs. Wilson, may I come in?"

Chapter 14

Karst entered the room behind Ashley. All of the women tensed as he walked into the room.

"Ladies," he said as he tipped his head towards them.

"Maybe we should leave so you and Detective Karst can have a visit," suggested Amy.

"No please stay," insisted Karst. "I'd like to visit with all of you, if that's okay with you."

Amy sat back down.

Karst studied the faces of all the Dolphins before he began.

"Mrs. Wilson," he began.

"Just call me Ashley," suggested Ashley.

"Okay, Ashley," continued Karst. "Were you aware that your husband had an accident yesterday?"

"Mark? He had an accident?" responded Ashley, trying to look more surprised than she was.

Karst checked the faces of the others and saw the same reaction. They were nervous but no one had the look of total shock on her face. No one seemed to care was the other point Karst took note of.

Ashley cleared her throat, "Um, is he alive?"

As soon as the words left her lips she regretted them. She should have asked if he was okay.

"Alive, yes, he's alive," replied Karst. "Why did you automatically assume he might be dead?"

"Well, you haven't exactly been the bearer of good news lately now, have you?" answered Ashley in an attempt to excuse her previous question.

"Please tell us what happened," asked Susan.

"Mr. Wilson and his daughter were at a construction site and she reportedly fell into the basement foundation of the house. Mr. Wilson called 911, and then tried to climb down to help her, and he fell as well. When the ambulance crew arrived, they found the two of them unconscious on the basement floor. Mr. Wilson regained consciousness this morning, but his daughter did not."

"How is Lexi?" asked Ashley with true concern in her voice.

"I heard the doctor tell Mr. Wilson that her vitals were good and they expected her to be fine," stated Karst.

Stephanie's eyes looked towards the package on the table.

Karst noticed the rest of the women were looking at the same package. He looked from them to the package

256

and back. All of his many years of instincts were telling him they were not surprised, they were all hiding something and that package meant something to them.

Before the conversation could continue any further, Karst received a call on his cell phone. He excused himself while he took the call. He stepped out of the room, but stood in a position that allowed him to see the women's images in a mirror hanging on the wall.

They began to frantically whisper to each other. Stephanie picked up the package and hid it in the top drawer of the desk. She returned to her seat on the sofa before Karst returned.

"Ladies there have been some details brought to my attention. According to the guys at the scene, there were signs of two struggles, one above the area where Lexi had fallen into the basement and the other at the site where Mr. Wilson had fallen in. I believe they were both pushed. I think it's time we have a serious conversation. Would you like to have it here or would you like to go downtown with me?"

"You couldn't possibly think one of us pushed them. Could you?" asked Amy.

Karst saw Amy's bandaged wrist. "What happened to your arm?" he asked.

"Oh, nothing, I had a small accident in my bathroom yesterday," she responded.

"Were you home all day yesterday?" asked Karst.

"Yes, until last night when we all went out to dinner. Why?"

"Can anyone vouch for your whereabouts late yesterday afternoon?" questioned Karst.

"No, I was home alone," answered Amy defensively.

"What about the rest of you?" asked Karst.

"I was home alone as well," answered Ashley.

"Same here," said Susan.

"Ditto," agreed Stephanie.

"So none of you can produce an alibi for your whereabouts yesterday afternoon," commented Karst.

"That's absolutely correct. We have nothing to hide, Detective Karst. Are you accusing one of us, or should I say, all of us as being involved with the struggles at the construction site?" demanded Amy, with her attorney instincts taking over.

"I'm not accusing anyone of anything just yet. I'm trying to get a complete picture here, so stay with me on this will ya?" he asked. "The real reason I'm here is to ask you ladies some questions from the past."

He flipped the pages of his notebook open to his copy of the chart he had on his wall.

He began, "I was concerned about the recent deaths of Mr. Wilson's two children and a possible connection. I did a little background work and found that some twenty years ago you ladies had an unfortunate spree of dead husbands. I'd like to ask you a few questions about all of that if I could."

"Aren't you going to read us our rights under the Miranda decision?" asked Amy with a very nasty tone to her voice.

"If you feel it's necessary, I'd be happy to," answered Karst.

"Just calm down," Susan said to Amy as she patted her on her knee. "Please continue Detective."

"Let me begin with the fact that you all went to school together and called yourselves the Dolphins? Correct?"

"Yes," answered Ashley.

"I'm assuming after high school all of you went off to college and married, but maintained your friendships? Am I still on the right track?" questioned Karst.

"Yes," answered Ashley once again.

"Then in the spring of 2000, Brittany, one of the Dolphins that is not here today, lost her husband in a construction site accident. That was followed by your husband Brian Saunders," he turned to Susan.

She nodded.

"Then, let's see, we have your husband shot to death in bed with another woman." He looked at Amy.

Amy nodded.

"Next you lost your husband to an explosion," he looked at Stephanie.

She nodded back.

259

"Your husband had an asthma attack. Then Mr. Wilson's wife, Theresa, was killed by a remote control airplane."

"Yes, I believe you have them in the correct order," agreed Ashley. "What's the point you are trying to make here?"

"Do all of you believe those deaths were accidents? Didn't it occur to any of you that it's not normal for a group the size of yours, living in different regions of the country, to each lose your husband within four months of each other?"

Ashley started to shake.

Stephanie stood up and began to pace.

Susan wrung her hands.

Amy just sat poker faced, waiting for Karst to go on.

"Ladies, I am prepared to begin a formal investigation into the deaths of your husbands unless you start talking now and have a pretty convincing reason why I shouldn't."

He saw the fear rising in them and wanted to move while they were frightened.

The women looked at each other. There was silence in the room while Karst waited for one of them to begin.

Amy started, "Detective Karst, I'm sure you've done your homework on all of these deaths and read the reports. They were all considered accidents except for the death of my husband. He got what he deserved, but you should also have read in the report that I wasn't even in the same city with him at the time of his death. I think you are trying to build a case where there is none."

"Why would you say they were 'considered' accidents instead of saying they were accidents?" asked Karst.

"Geez, Susan, he thinks he's a shrink like you, trying to catch me on some Freudian slip," complained Amy as she walked across the room to make herself a drink. "Would anyone like to join me?"

They all declined, but were concerned if Amy began drinking her mouth might get them into trouble.

Karst continued with his questioning, "Mrs. Wilson, er Ashley, I'm aware that after Mr. Wilson lost his wife, the two of you were married. Would you care to explain the circumstances surrounding that?"

Stephanie piped in, "There's nothing to explain. They dated while in high school, married other people and got back together when they each lost their partners. There's nothing new to that, it happens all the time."

Karst turned to Ashley again.

"I hate to say this but I've noticed your connection to death is greater than the average person. I was here for your husband's death, I was here when Mr. Saunders died, and then there was your nanny and more recently Mr. Wilson's two kids. Now your husband and his other

261

daughter are in the hospital. I'm afraid it's not going to look good for you."

Karst could tell Ashley was the weak link in the group by her apparent show of emotion. He was glad she was the one that had the most connections. He felt he could break her more easily.

Ashley started to cry.

Susan jumped to her side.

"I think we've answered enough of your questions for today, Detective," said Susan.

Ashley could not take it. She sobbed, "I can't keep this secret any longer. It's going to kill me."

The others went to her to try to calm her and quiet her from speaking any more.

Susan looked back at Karst to see his reaction. He knew they were definitely hiding something after that outburst. He was pleased with himself, but wasn't convinced they had anything to do with the murders.

Amy stepped forward. "Girls, I think we've covered for Theresa long enough. Maybe we should tell Detective Karst what she did."

They all turned to look at Amy.

They took Amy's lead. They could get the story out and not have to include themselves or Mark in the equation. They could explain the deaths, name the murderer and stay safe.

Susan began. She told Karst how badly they all treated Theresa when she got pregnant and married Mark missing the opportunity to go to college. She explained how Ashley and Theresa met again, how the slumber party came to be and finally the drunken recording of them at the party planning murders of their husbands to help Ashley with new plots for her books.

Stephanie picked it up from there. She explained how Theresa took the tape and sent them copies of their song. She put Theresa at the scene of each and every murder. She explained how mentally unstable Theresa was.

Amy took over. She gave Karst their reasons from a legal point of view why they never went to the police, about how they were afraid they'd be implicated. How they attempted to stop the murders. She told him about the others blaming her at one point and how they drugged her to stop the killings. When Ashley's husband died while Amy was drugged, they confirmed Theresa was behind all of the deaths. While they were trying to figure out how to handle her, their problem was solved. One day the remote control plane she was flying accidentally killed her. After that, they thought there was no point in going to the police. Until now, the police never knew about all of the deaths from different cities or that there was any type of connection.

Karst listened intently to the women and their accounts of what happened. Strange as it all sounded, he believed them. Now he wondered what to do with his newfound information. Theresa was already dead; he couldn't arrest her and convict her of the murders.

"Ladies, I'll be back. Let me give some thought to what you've told me. I want to thank you for coming clean and answering my questions. I'll let you know how I plan to proceed with the information from here."

"Ashley, I'm sure you'd like to go visit your husband now. I hope his daughter regains consciousness soon," he said as he left the room to let himself out.

Stephanie went to the window to watch Karst drive away.

"Whew, good save, Amy!" announced Stephanie as she returned to the room.

"I was rather ingenious if I do say so myself. I think I deserve another drink," remarked Amy.

"Now what?" asked Ashley. "Do you think he bought the whole story? I guess most of what we told him was true. We just left out the part that we found out years later Mark was the killer not Theresa."

"Knowing Karst the way I do, I'd say we bought some time and that's about it. Sooner or later he's going to try to connect the recent deaths to those from the past. It's inevitable. In the meantime, it'll give us a chance to work out the details of the next chapter we feed to him. We need to be as convincing as we were today; we have to be in total agreement on what we'll say," warned Amy.

"I think we'd better figure out who's behind what's happening now. It's kinda scary thinking if it's not Mark, someone else is out on the lose killing people," commented Susan.

"I guess I'd better play the concerned wife and head off to the hospital to visit Mark. I don't want Karst getting any more suspicious than he already is. Can you believe him? He thought I was somehow responsible for all the deaths," groaned Ashley.

"Hey, I'm telling ya, you're not out of the woods yet. He's still going to try to connect you to the recent deaths. Mark my words," said Amy raising her glass.

"Why don't you go over to the hospital, and we'll stay here a while longer where it's private and plot our next strategy," suggested Stephanie.

Ashley took her advice and went to visit Mark.

When Karst returned to his office, Kent was not there. He was relieved. He wasn't sure what to tell him yet. He needed to unravel more facts about the old and the new cases.

He pulled out all of the files again. He had the files from the out of state deaths sent to him so he could study them. He followed closely the notes he had written down as the girls were telling him their story. He wanted to compare facts.

He was surprised, after all of the years that had passed, the girls had the facts down pretty accurately. That reinforced his idea that they were telling him the truth, or at least, they were well rehearsed.

He listed all the players involved. He searched the files for alibis and began to piece together the story just as they had told him. He now understood how the other girls might have thought Amy was to blame. Along with Theresa, she had access to all the murdered victims except her own husband. That one could actually have been an isolated murder not connected in any way to the others.

His thoughts turned to Amy. Did they really cover all the bases? If Michael had really died of an asthma attack while Amy was drugged and there was not foul play, she still could be the killer. She, unlike Theresa, is still around today. She could be continuing on her killing spree.

Frantically, Karst began to sort through the papers writing notes.

"Wow," he whispered, "it could actually be Judge Roth that committed all those murders and is still going strong. Maybe blaming Ashley was barking up the wrong tree."

He sat back in his chair, tipped his head back, and thought about the individual girls and their behavior earlier in the day. He remembered how angry Amy was, and it was a surprise to him to watch the way she could drink. There's some definite underlying bitterness going on there. Not to mention her reputation in the courtroom for being a real hardass. Suddenly, as if someone hit him

with a hard object, the picture of Amy's hand in a bandage
came into Karst's mind.

"The bandage," he muttered. "She said she hurt
her hand yesterday. The struggle with Mr. Wilson and his
daughter happened yesterday. I wonder what's really
going on under that bandage?"

Just then Kent walked in. He looked at all the files
scattered in total disarray on Karst's desk. This was so
out of character for Karst and his tidy habits that Kent
knew in a moment that he was on to something that
rushed him through the files, not allowing him enough
time to keep them in tidy stacks.

Karst looked up at Kent. He knew he'd been
caught.

"What'd you find?" asked Kent excitedly.

"Sit down Kent. We've gotta talk."

"You did discover something, didn't you? Are the
deaths related? Were any of them not accidents?" quizzed
Kent breathlessly.

"I really didn't want to share this with you. I
thought you were too close to the case. If I tell you what
I've learned so far will you keep your mouth shut until I
tell you otherwise?"

"Sure boss, you know I'll do whatever you ask."

"I went to talk to Ashley today. When I got there
your mom, and the rest of the Dolphins were there. I went
to inform her that her husband was in the hospital..."
started Karst.

267

Kent interrupted, "Wait, what do you mean her husband's in the hospital? What happened? Is he okay?"

Karst explained, "This morning I went to the hospital when I heard two people were brought in that had an accidental fall. When I learned the names of the patients, I thought I would pay Mr. Wilson a call and ask him a few questions. He told me his daughter had fallen into the basement foundation of this house they were building. He said he called 911 and then he must've fallen in himself while trying to climb down to help her. He had no memory of the fall or anything else until he woke up in the hospital. He said they were alone at the scene."

"Wow, that's too bad. Is he going to make it? What about his daughter, Lexi?" questioned Kent.

"I think they're both going to be okay," Karst reassured him.

"I'm sorry. I interrupted you. Go on with what you were starting to tell me," apologized Kent.

"As I was saying," Karst began again. "All of the women were at Ashley's house when I arrived to tell her the news. Since they were all together, I took advantage of the opportunity to begin asking them questions about the deaths of their husbands. At first they acted like they knew nothing about what I was getting at. Ashley was very shook up. Judge Roth became a little, shall I say, hostile."

"Kent, I'm not sure if I should be telling you this. I might be out of line. Maybe you should talk to your mother about it. Maybe you should hear it from her."

"Just tell me what you know," insisted Kent.

"It's not too pretty, but here goes," Karst sighed. "Seems there was no love lost between Theresa, the original Mrs. Wilson, and the rest of the Dolphins. I guess they all turned their backs on her. They all had gone on to receive top-notch educations and had successful careers while Theresa was home with three kids and a husband with a job that could barely meet their needs. She was livid with jealousy."

"Mrs. Wilson, no, that's confusing, Ashley met her at a book signing and they decided to get the others together to renew their friendship. They threw a slumber party for old times. They got drunk. During the party they played a game where they plotted the deaths of their own husbands in such a way that Ashley could use the stories for her murder mysteries."

"I don't get it," said Kent.

"Let me go on," insisted Karst. "It seems they tape recorded the conversation about the murder plots. Now here's where it gets ugly. Theresa was mentally off. She played the scenarios through. Kent, she killed all those people."

"Oh, come on. You've got to be kidding. How could she be so cold-hearted? I don't believe it," argued Kent.

"Believe it, my boy, that's the story I got from all the women. I've been digging through all the facts here and their story works. Except for...

"Except for what?" begged Kent.

"Well all the pieces of the puzzle fit, except there could be two ways to build the puzzle. After going over all the facts, something that Judge Roth said made me wonder. I went back over the material and it's possible there were two people that could be suspects. Not just Theresa," explained Karst.

Now Kent was really getting into it. "Who? Who killed my dad?" demanded Kent.

"Give me a minute here, I haven't finished my research yet. I don't want to mislead you. For all intents and purposes it's probably safe to believe the story the women gave me is accurate. If you feel up to it, you can help me sort through the facts and confirm that it was Theresa," suggested Karst.

"Are you sure you're up to this?" quizzed Karst. "After all this is your dad we're talking about. Looks like his death wasn't an accident after all. You seem pretty calm about it all."

"I never knew my dad. Remember?" reminded Kent. "I came along after his death. All I know about him were the stories my mom told me. I guess she couldn't tell me the truth, so she's kept this to herself for all of these years."

Kent sat still, thinking about his mother.

270

"She must feel such relief now having this out in the open. Tonight I'll spent some time with her so we can talk about it."

"I guess if you never really knew him, it's understandable that you could take this as well as you appear to," said Karst.

"You said you had some research to do here, so let's get started," suggested Kent.

"Okay, we need to read through all the interviews about Ashley's first husband, Michael. We need to find out if his death could have been an accident not a murder," explained Karst.

"Why?" quizzed Kent. "What difference would that make? If Theresa killed all the others, why does finding out she didn't kill one make any difference?"

"If I can prove she didn't kill this one, I may have a second suspect remember? If we prove Michael was killed and it was not an accident then my other suspect is cleared," explained Karst.

"I want to know right now who you think the other suspect could be," demanded Kent once again.

"Okay, but it's an unproven theory at this point. The women at one time thought Judge Roth could've committed the murders and they cleared her because they had her drugged when Mr. Moore died. She couldn't have done it," stated Karst.

"I don't believe that for one minute. She's not the type," Kent said in her defense.

271

"Well then help me prove my theory wrong. Let's put this case to rest so we can focus on the deaths and accidents surrounding Mr. Wilson. I'd like to get home at a decent time tonight," insisted Karst.

When Ashley arrived at the hospital, Mark was sitting on the edge of his bed, dressed and ready to go home.

"What are you doing? Surely they haven't released you yet, have they?" asked Ashley.

"No, but they can't keep me here either. I'm leaving. I was going to call a cab, but since you're here, get me out of here. I have to find out who's hurting my kids," replied Mark.

"Okay, okay. I'll take you home. We have to talk. I guess the car would be more private than here anyway," answered Ashley.

She helped Mark out to the nurse's station where, after some arguing with the nurses, they let him sign himself out. His injuries consisted of a broken arm, lots of bumps and bruises, and a horrendous headache.

On the way home in the car, Ashley explained everything to Mark about the visit from Karst earlier and their confession.

"Are you sure he is convinced Theresa killed everyone and we're all off of the hook?" asked Mark.

"I guess. At least he told us he believed us," Ashley reassured him.

"You girls handled it great. Thanks. Now we need to find out who's trying to kill me. I didn't tell Karst the whole story, but my guess is, Lexi was pushed into the basement. I went off to relieve myself and when I came back I saw her lying there. I ran to get some tarp straps to lower myself down to her. Someone hit me over the head and knocked me silly. I tried to fight off whoever it was. I lost my gun in the struggle. Last thing I remember was being pushed and falling, then waking up in the hospital," reported Mark.

"Could you tell who it was?" asked Ashley.

"No, I couldn't even tell if it was a man or a woman. The attacker had his or her face covered with a stocking hat or mask or something. I'm unclear about that, my vision was blurred from the blow to my head," explained Mark.

Later that night, Mark couldn't sleep. His arm and whole body ached. He couldn't find a comfortable position. He went down to his basement shop. He thought he could find something to do down there to keep his mind off his pain.

He was listening to music and reading a book when he heard the shuffle of footsteps in the shadows.

"Ashley, is that you?" he called out towards the sound as he struggled to stand up.

He strained his eyes to look into the dark shadows at the other end of the room. A figure stepped out into the dim light.

"You? What are you doing here? No! Don't!" screamed Mark as the bullet shot across the room hitting him squarely in his heart. Mark was dead before he hit the floor.

Chapter 15

It was the middle of the night. The street in front of Ashley's house was alive with activity. There were lights flashing and people coming and going from the house in every direction. Ashley's yard lights added to the strange lighting for so late at night.

When Karst arrived on the scene, Ashley's friends were already there. Kent was among the group surrounding Ashley on the front lawn. She was wrapped in a blanket, and refused to go back inside until Mark's body was removed from her house.

Downstairs, a team of crime scene investigators was scouring the basement shop area for anything they could use. They were lifting fingerprints, and searching for the casing from the bullet that killed Mark.

The body could not be released, or moved until Karst had a chance to see it in its original position, on the floor.

Karst surveyed the area, and nodded clearance. Mark's body was removed from the scene.

Karst went back outside to talk with Ashley.

"Did you check the house? Is someone hiding in there?" asked a terrified Ashley.

"Ashley, we've got a crew in there checking every inch of the house. I think it's safe to assume there's no one in there. Would you like to step back inside?" Karst asked her.

"Come on Ash, let's go inside. I'm sure it's safe now," pleaded Susan.

The ladies gathered around Ashley, and took her indoors.

Karst turned to Kent, "What the hell happened in there?"

"I'm not sure. Ashley is pretty shaken up," replied Kent.

"Well, let's go hear her story," sighed Karst.

Part of him felt he was moving too slowly on all of this. People were dropping like flies. He thought if he had been working harder, maybe some of these deaths and accidents could have been prevented. Karst had always been so confident that he was doing his job to the best of his ability, but something about this mess really got to him in a big way.

Susan was sitting on the sofa next to Ashley. Stephanie was just returning from the kitchen with a cup of tea for her. Karst and Kent walked in.

"Where's Judge Roth?" asked Karst, noticing she was the only one missing.

"I'm here," said Amy as she walked into the living room. "What in the hell happened? Who shot Mark?"

Stephanie set the tea down on the coffee table. She went to Amy, who had just arrived on the scene. "Ashley heard a gunshot, and pushed her panic button in her room. Then she called us. She locked herself in until the police got here," explained Stephanie.

"How did you know Mark had been shot?" Karst questioned Amy.

"I saw them carrying a body out, so I asked. Ashley called me and said she heard a gunshot, so I knew it wasn't her. The only other person living here was Mark. Even if I hadn't asked the guys outside I would've assumed it was Mark," snapped Amy showing little patience that night for Detective Karst.

"I'd like to visit with each of you in private. Please stay in this room until I send for you and please refrain from any discussions."

Karst turned to Ashley. "Would you come with me please?"

After they were seated in the kitchen Karst began, "Where were you when you heard the gunshot?"

"I was in my room. I couldn't sleep. I was reading. I heard a loud sound coming from the basement. At first I wasn't sure what it was, but then when I thought about it for a moment, I thought it could've been a gunshot. I didn't want to go check it out myself, so I pushed my panic button and waited for the police to come," explained Ashley.

"You also called your friends," reminded Karst.

"Yes, after I knew the police would be arriving, I called them. I didn't want to be alone," replied Ashley.

"Then what happened?"

"Well, nothing really. When the police got here, I ran down and let them in. Then I ran outside because I was afraid to stay in the house.

"Stephanie was the first to arrive, and then Susan, then Kent and now Amy is here," said Ashley.

"Did you go downstairs and identify Mark's body?" asked Karst.

"No, Kent did it for me when he got here," responded Ashley.

"Were you and Mr. Wilson the only two people in the house tonight?" began Karst.

"Yes," replied Ashley.

"Wait a minute, I thought Mr. Wilson was in the hospital," quizzed Karst.

"He was, but when I went to see him he insisted they release him and I brought him back here late this afternoon," reported Ashley.

"So no one else was in the house except you and Mr. Wilson. You were in your room; you heard a shot, set off the house alarm and waited for the police and your friends to arrive. Is that about it? Ashley answered, "Yes, that's the way it happened."

278

"If no one was in the house but you and Mr. Wilson, why do you suppose your alarm didn't go off when the intruder entered? Do you think Mr. Wilson knew the attacker and let that person in the house tonight?" quizzed Karst.

"I suppose that's possible, but I would've thought I'd have heard the bell if someone came to the door," answered Ashley.

"But Mr. Wilson could've, say, talked to someone on the phone and expected a visitor, letting him or her in? Is that possible?" asked Karst.

"I guess, but that wouldn't be like Mark. Most of his friends and acquaintances are in New York. He really didn't have a social life here. I'd say he didn't let the shooter in," commented Ashley.

"You always set your alarm, don't you? Why didn't the alarm go off if neither you nor Mr. Wilson let someone in intentionally?" questioned Karst.

"I don't know why the alarm didn't go off. It was set to go off. I check it every night before I go to bed," said Ashley.

"Do you think Mr. Wilson went out tonight and forgot to turn it back on? Could he have gone out for a drink, or to buy something, or just to take a walk?" asked Karst.

"No, Mark was in a great deal of pain from his accident. He had everything here that he needed. He would've had trouble driving and it would've hurt too much to take a walk. He had a lot of trouble just getting into my car when I brought him home from the hospital. He moved very slowly and the pain was only tolerable while he was on his pain medication. I was surprised to find out that he went to the basement at all," remarked Ashley.

"Well, someone got into the house without setting off the alarm, shot Mr. Wilson, and fled before the police arrived. There was no sign of forced entry according to the guys checking out the house tonight. Who has keys to your house besides you and Mr. Wilson?" questioned Karst.

She hated to drag them into this, but she had no choice.

"All of my friends here have a key. We all have keys to each other's houses. We have for years," explained Ashley.

"Do all of them know the code for the alarm system?" asked Karst.

"It's written on the tag that the keys are clipped to," explained Ashley.

"Can you think of anyone else that had a key to your house?" quizzed Karst, hoping she had forgotten someone.

"No, except Carol, but she returned the key on her last day," said Ashley.

"Carol, she was your housekeeper or secretary."

"Did you part on good terms or did you have to fire her?" asked Karst.

"Oh no, we parted on very good terms. Carol would never do anything like this. No, not Carol."

"Now, Ashley, did Mr. Wilson have any enemies? Can you come up with anyone that wanted to hurt him or his kids?" asked Karst.

"No," lied Ashley.

"Do you have anything else to add?" asked Karst.

"No, I've told you everything."

"Ashley, I'm going to ask that you allow us to check your hands for gunshot residue. Is that okay with you? Since you were the only two in the house, this is just routine."

Karst sent Ashley to be tested, and sent Kent to bring Stephanie to the kitchen.

"How'd you know to come here tonight?" asked Karst as he looked up at Kent standing behind his mother with his hand on her shoulder.

"Mom called me from her cell phone as she was driving over. I jumped out of bed and headed right over. Actually, I continued talking to her as she drove over, explaining to her not to touch anything until the police got here. Once she told me she was at the house and Ashley was okay we hung up our phones and I arrived a little while later," explained Kent.

"Where's Ashley?" asked Stephanie.

"I sent her off to have a gunshot residue test," said Karst.

"Now wait one minute," exploded Stephanie. "You don't think Ashley killed Mark, do you?"

"Mom, cool it. It's better for Ashley if she just lets them check it out and go on with the investigation, ruling her out as a suspect," explained Kent.

"You know, since all of you are tied so closely together with your death experiences from the past, it might be a good idea for each of you to be tested, just to rule out any doubt," suggested Karst.

"I think that's a good idea," echoed Kent.

After they were in agreement about being tested, Karst went on with his questioning.

Karst sat back on the chair he was sitting on. He tried to make himself comfortable he knew he would be staying until he got the whole story.

"Kent," said Karst. "I think I need to speak with the other ladies alone. Why don't you check with the crew outside and let me know if they find anything we can use."

Kent's face showed definite disappointment. He felt Karst was treating him like a child that shouldn't be in the room while his parents are having a serious conversation.

Kent walked his mother out to be tested and sent Susan into the kitchen.

Karst began, "What can you tell me about what's going on here?"

Susan started, "Well, sir there's more to the story than we told you. We told you Theresa killed all of our husbands. And that's what we thought for years and years. Then, one day, Mark confided in Ashley that he was the one that had killed everyone. He wanted to be free of Theresa. The idea came to him after he heard our tape from the party. He followed through on the murders and allowed us to think it was Theresa all along."

"He kept us quiet by threatening to drag us in with him as accomplices. He had us over a barrel. We couldn't bring our husbands back by exposing him, and going down with him could ruin our lives, so we kept the secret to ourselves."

"We were accepting it and our lives were moving on until recently," admitted Susan. "Someone killed Trystan, then Isha. Whoever it was, sent Mark copies of the tape referring only to the method of death that was used with each of his kids. Mark knew someone was killing his kids. He told Ashley that he was pushed at the house site, and so was Lexi. He said he struggled with his attacker, but lost. Before you came to tell Ashley about Mark being in the hospital, a package arrived with a CD in it with Brittany's voice describing her husband's death at his construction site. Then Mark and Lexi were attacked at a construction site."

"Where are these CDs now?" asked Karst.

"The one that came last is in a drawer in the other room," said Susan. Karst went with her to retrieve the package.

Karst recognized the package as the one Stephanie had hidden when he was last there to interview them.

One by one he finished his interviews of the Dolphins then returned to the living room where the ladies were waiting.

"May I listen to this," asked Karst holding up the CD he had removed from the package. He went to the entertainment center to play it.

"Sure, I guess, if you have to," said Ashley.

Kent walked into the room when the CD was finished. He carried a plastic bag with him that contained another CD.

"This was found near Mark's body on the floor," explained Kent.

Karst took the bag. He opened it. He carefully used his pen to remove the CD. He held it to the light to look for fingerprints. There were none. He put it into the player to listen.

He looked up at Kent and tipped his head towards the door, asking him to leave again.

Kent was still annoyed about being left out of the investigation but he obediently headed back outside to wait.

Karst pushed play. This time the voice was that of Amy's talking about shooting Jonathon.

"Mark was shot," gasped Susan.

Karst removed the CD from the player and dropped it back into the evidence bag.

"I'm going to leave you ladies now. If you can come up with anything I can use, please contact me. I'm sure you know this is not over. I'm sorry to say you're all very tightly woven into this mess. I expect all of you to remain easy to reach until we make some sense of this."

Karst went outside to find Kent. He told him he was finished there and was going back to the office. He'd see him there.

Later that morning, Karst was called into his sergeant's office.

"What'd you find out about that shooting this morning?" he asked.

"I've just begun to start getting some of the reports. Someone supposedly got into the house without setting off the alarm and shot the husband while the wife was upstairs. She heard the gunshot and set off the alarm and waited for help to arrive," responded Karst.

"Is it true that the Nolan kid you've been working with is somehow connected to the victim? There's been talk around the office this morning," he demanded.

"Well, his mother is a friend of the wife," Karst started. "Oh hell, there's so much more to this case than one dead husband. I think I can link that group of women to six dead husbands, a dead wife and two dead kids. I'm so close to fitting it all together. If only I had finished putting the pieces together, I might have been able to prevent this guy from being shot."

"Get Thompson on this with you and send that kid back to patrol. It's time anyway. He's been hanging around here long enough. I've been getting some static about it. He has no business working this case if his family is involved," he said.

"Absolutely," agreed Karst knowing this all along but hoping to use him as long as possible for information. "I'll tell him today when he comes in. I'll go fill in Thompson."

On his way back to his office, Karst found Thompson and asked him to come to his office.

When Thompson arrived Karst began to fill him in on all of the details.

Kent walked into the office and saw Thompson going through the files. He felt rejected after the way he was treated last night at the scene, and now this hurt even more. He wanted to be the one to help Karst crack this case.

Karst motioned with his head for Thompson to step out of the room.

"I'm sorry, Kent, but I got the word this morning to take you off of this case. I really am sorry. You've been great help on this. I couldn't have gotten this far without you. You're gonna make one hell of a detective after you pay your dues and put in your time. I can promise you that. I'll also promise to do anything I can when the time comes to help you make detective."

The disappointment on Kent's face was impossible to hide. His eyes began to well with tears, but he managed to choke them back.

"I worked so hard. I really hoped you would be able to keep me on. I really wanted to break the old cases, and show you how good of a detective I could be," confided Kent.

"Hey, you did great work, but the time is not right. You shouldn't be working on a case involving your family. You're young and you have your whole future ahead of you on the force," replied Karst, feeling Kent's pain.

Kent quickly left the room; he bumped into Thompson as he passed by him. He didn't say a word he just kept going.

Thompson asked, "How'd the kid take it?"

"Not very well, not very well," replied Karst as he watched Kent until he was out of sight.

"Okay, let's get back to work," suggested Thompson.

Together they covered all the evidence they had on all the cases. The gun from Mark's murder was not at the scene nor was the shell casing. They were still waiting for the reports to come back to help clear the women or accuse them if they were involved.

"From what you've told me so far, and by going over these files, it's pretty damn obvious it's one of the women. Are any of them remarried?" asked Thompson.

"Well, Kent's mom is. Why, what are you getting at?" asked Karst.

"If he's living with her, he had access to the key. Don't you think we have to add him to the list of suspects? Did he know this Mark guy? Would he have any reason to think his wife might be in danger?" questioned Thompson.

"Come to think of it, he didn't show up with his wife. He let her leave the house in the middle of the night and go to a murder scene alone. That does seem a little odd, doesn't it? I mean, I sure as hell wouldn't let Debbie run right into the middle of a mess like that," stated Karst.

"I'd say let's go pay a visit to Nolan's mom and step dad," suggested Thompson.

They knocked on the door, but there was no answer. As they were about to leave, Stephanie pulled her car into the driveway.

Karst introduced Thompson to her and jumped right into the questions.

"Is your husband home?" asked Karst.

"No, I just dropped him off at the airport. He was called away this morning," she replied. "Why?"

"This call, was it for business?" asked Thompson.

"No, he's retired. He was asked to sub at some golf tournament in LA. One of the guys got pretty sick and he's on the sub list," explained Stephanie.

"Isn't it kind of long trip for a last minute golf tournament?" questioned Thompson.

"Oh, not if you know Alex," laughed Stephanie. "He flies anywhere on a moment's notice. I'm pretty used to it by now."

"Does your husband know Mr. Wilson?" asked Karst.

"No, they'd never met," responded Stephanie beginning to get nervous.

"I'm gonna cut right to the chase," began Karst. "Does he know the story about Mr. Wilson and all of the deaths?"

"Yes, I told him everything before we were married. I've kept him informed about everything that's been happening," admitted Stephanie not liking the way the conversation was headed.

"Why didn't he turn Mark in?" asked Thompson.

"He wanted to. I begged him not to. I convinced him that could damage too many lives. He promised to keep our secret."

"Does he have access to your keys to Ashley's house?" Thompson questioned.

"I suppose so. I just keep them in a basket on the hall table."

"Are they there now?" asked Thompson.

"Probably," said Stephanie as she unlocked her door and went inside.

The two men followed her to the basket but the keys were not there.

Stephanie looked up at the men with a frightened, surprised look on her face.

"Could the keys be anywhere else?" asked Karst.

"No," replied Stephanie, wishing the answer could have been yes.

"We'll need all of the information you can give us about your husband's itinerary please," insisted Karst.

After Stephanie gave them the information, they left.

"Looks like we have another suspect to add to that list of yours," stated Thompson.

"So this Alex guy knew about Mark. Then he...wait a minute," said Karst as he jumped out of the car and ran back to the door.

Stephanie came to the door.

"Did your husband have access to a copy of the taped voices from the party?" quizzed Karst.

Once again Stephanie was not happy with the answer she had to give.

"Yes, we all have copies. We thought it would be safer in case anything happened to any one of us, the others would still have a copy of the taped conversation to use against Mark if he tried to harm any of us," explained Stephanie.

"What'd you find out?" quizzed Thompson.

"Now we know he and all of the women have a copy of that tape. Any one of them could have made the recordings," reported Karst.

"Any chance they are all in this together?" asked Thompson.

"To tell you the truth, I'd believe almost anything at this point," admitted Karst.

Stephanie was so upset about what she had to tell the detectives. She called Kent to get his opinion on how the case was going. He didn't answer his phone. Stephanie thought that was a bit odd, as Kent always kept his cell phone with him. Maybe he's interviewing someone or can't talk now, she thought to herself. She then called Ashley.

The women got together that night and went out to dinner, to talk about Mark's death and to get Ashley out of that house. During the evening, Stephanie tried to reach Kent again so he could fill them in on the details; still no answer.

The next morning, Karst stopped by to see Kent. He still felt badly about sending him back and wanted to see how he was taking it. He was surprised to hear he was a no-show at work that morning. He knew he shouldn't have gotten emotionally attached to him, but he still felt close to Kent, like he would if he'd had a son of his own.

He called his cell phone but there was no answer. He called his mother.

"No, I can't reach him either," was the response from Stephanie when Karst called. "Isn't he with you?"

"I had to stop him from working on the case because of being too close to all of you. I'm afraid he took it pretty hard. I was hoping to talk with him this morning to see how he was doing, but he didn't show up at work. Maybe I'll stop by his place. I'm sure he's fine, just not in a very talkative mood," Karst said, trying to reassure Stephanie.

"How about if I meet you there. I need to know he's okay myself," suggested Stephanie.

"Okay, I'll meet you there in about thirty minutes," agreed Karst.

Karst was at Kent's door when Stephanie arrived.

"His car's here, but he's not answering the door," said Karst.

"Kent, open up. It's mom. Let us in," she called through the door as she knocked.

They waited, but there was no answer.

"I can hear music playing, do you suppose he's ignoring us?" asked Karst.

"Who knows? He can get pretty moody sometimes. I'll just use my key," answered Stephanie as she put her key in the door.

They walked in.

"Kent. Kent are you in here?" called Stephanie from the livingroom.

There was still no response.

Karst's instincts were up.

"Wait here. Don't go any further," he told her.

Karst went from room to room looking for Kent. When he opened the door to Kent's computer room, he saw Kent's body slumped over his desk. A gun lay on the floor. His blood had spilled across the top of the desk and pooled on the floor.

"Is he in there?" yelled Stephanie from the livingroom where she obediently waited.

"Stay there," he called back.

He dialed 911 on his phone then went to Stephanie.

"Come here and sit down," he said to her, guiding her to the sofa.

"What's wrong? Something's wrong with Kent. I need to go to him." She tried to get up but Detective Karst insisted she stay seated.

"I'm sorry, but Kent's been shot," he told her.

"Is he okay? Let's go help him. Did you call for help?" she asked, frantically trying to get past Karst to go to him.

"I'm sorry, but it's too late. He's gone. He's been dead for a number of hours now," explained Karst.

She fell into his arms sobbing.

A group of officers entered the house along with an ambulance crew. They looked at Karst holding Stephanie in his arms. He motioned with his head in the direction of the room where Kent was.

"Get Thompson here," Karst told one of the officers. He knew he was not up to handling this at the moment. He, too, was choking back tears about Kent's death.

Karst walked Stephanie out to his car. He drove her to Ashley's house and walked her to the door.

Ashley answered the door.

"Kent's been shot," he told Ashley. "She's not in very good shape. I need to get back over there."

Ashley could tell Karst was not himself. He handed Stephanie off to her and went back to the house.

When he walked back into Kent's house, one of the officers at the scene took him aside and said, "There's something in there you need to check out."

Karst was distraught over Kent's death. He somehow knew his death was connected to the rest of the murders surrounding his mother and her friends.

He took a deep breath, and went back inside to go to work. He walked into the room where Kent's body remained slumped over the desk. One of the officers pointed to the gun on the floor.

The gun had an evidence tag on it. There was a baggy with a shell casing inside marked " Mark Wilson murder". There were clothes hanging neatly in the closet, each with an evidence tag attached.

Karst walked over to them. One was a mechanic's uniform marked "Trystan Wilson's case", next was a uniform from the gas company with the tag marked "Isha Wilson's case". Next to them hung black clothes including a stocking mask. All of those items were marked "Lexi Wilson's case".

One of the officers handed Karst an envelope with his name on it.

I knew you'd be the one to find me. I'm sorry I disappointed you. I really couldn't decide if I would make a better criminal than a detective so I had to try both. I feel I failed at each. Kent.